MLO

The familiar handsomeness sent shivers racking through her.

The high cheekbones, full lips and his imposing height reminded her, as they always had, of drawings of potent Japanese emperors with long swords from centuries gone by. Especially in the shadow profile of the light shining down on him, he commanded all he surveyed. His dark hair still fell in a thick, youthful tousle downward from his forehead, hinting at a rebelliousness despite the fine navy suit perfectly tailored to his lean, muscular body.

As if knowing she'd be there, he turned his head. His almost-black, gleaming eyes bore into hers the instant they made contact, causing her breath to shorten, and she went from a casual pose to standing at attention.

Slowly, the seriousness in his face melted to something gentler, where it lingered for a moment. Then the gaze quickly corrected itself, as if the previous move had been a swiftly caught error. He returned to his piercing stare. Kento Yamamoto bowed his head and said only, "It's good to see you again, Erin."

Dear Reader,

With this book I got to incorporate two things I love. The first was to enjoy the sights, smells and sounds of an exciting locale. I think Seattle is a knockout of a city. Greenery is squeezed into everywhere a metropolis will allow, and the frequent rain keeps it lush. It's easy to figure out how the nickname Emerald City came to be. Add to that a rich heritage of international culture, which is reflected in the neighborhoods, art, music and food. What's more, a wild history of fires and gold rushes and scandals. I've visited there a few times and hope to return again soon.

Another element I love about this book is the reunion story. Kento and Erin come back together with complete misunderstandings about what had happened between them in the past. They're both absolutely certain that the wounds they inflicted on each other could never heal. But when the truth comes out, we get to watch them begin to move forward. Is it too late for their love?

As always, thanks so much for reading.

Andrea x

Wedding Date with the Billionaire

Andrea Bolter

HARLEQUIN®

Romance™

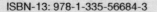

Recycling programs for this product may not exist in your area.

ISBN-13: 978-1-335-56684-3

Wedding Date with the Billionaire

Copyright © 2021 by Andrea Bolter

This edition published by arrangement with Harlequin Books S.A.

For questions and comments about the quality of this book, please contact us at CustomerService@Harlequin.com.

Harlequin Enterprises ULC
22 Adelaide St. West, 40th Floor
Toronto, Ontario M5H 4E3, Canada
www.Harlequin.com

Printed in U.S.A.

Andrea Bolter has always been fascinated by matters of the heart. In fact, she's the one her girlfriends turn to for advice with their love lives. A city mouse, she lives in Los Angeles with her husband and daughter. She loves travel, rock 'n' roll, sitting at cafés and watching romantic comedies she's already seen a hundred times. Say hi at andreabolter.com.

Books by Andrea Bolter

Harlequin Romance

Her New York Billionaire
Her Las Vegas Wedding
The Italian's Runaway Princess
The Prince's Cinderella
His Convenient New York Bride
Captivated by Her Parisian Billionaire

Visit the Author Profile page at Harlequin.com.

For Linda

Praise for
Andrea Bolter

CHAPTER ONE

"LADIES." KENTO YAMAMOTO stood on the boat dock and bowed his head to one then the other of the overly perfumed females who had just flanked him, a blonde on one side and a brunette on the other.

"How are you, Kento?" the blonde asked in a high-pitched tone.

"We've missed you," cooed the brunette.

He'd met the two years ago but, for the life of him, couldn't remember their names. It was hard to fathom that they'd *missed* him when he barely knew who they were.

"Isn't it exciting, Christy and Lucas's wedding?" The brunette stated the obvious. "And you're going to be the best man!"

"You came all the way from Tokyo to stand up for Lucas," the blonde chimed in, as if he was unaware of where he lived. "You're such a good friend!"

"Yeah, he's lucky to have a good friend like you."

"Yeah."

"Yeah."

Kento responded with a tight-lipped smile, already done with this superficial chitchat. He'd been about to board the small private yacht he'd chartered for the ride across Seattle's Puget Sound to Willminson Island for the wedding weekend of his oldest friend. Then the two bubbly girls, friends of the bride's, if he recalled correctly, recognized him and came clamoring toward him, clomping down the wooden dock on their high heels even in Seattle's misty weather.

"We were just about to take the state ferry." The brunette pointed to the next dock over, where the enormous vessel that transported tourists and residents the quick half hour to the island was loading. "And then MacKenzie spotted you, so we came running over to say hi."

Aha. The blonde's name was MacKenzie. One down.

"Amber said we just *had* to!"

"Had to." MacKenzie giggled.

Blonde, MacKenzie. Brunette was Amber.

Noted. Kento didn't wonder why they just *had* to rush over to say hi. It wasn't because they were actually old friends gathering to celebrate the nuptials of two of their inner circle. No, it was because women like these two were professional money sniffers and had no doubt heard that Kento Yamamoto, the Seattle-born Japanese American billionaire who made his fortune in Tokyo, would be in attendance.

"How have you been?" MacKenzie asked through her awful bright orange lipstick.

"What's Japan like?" came Amber's probe with a sweep of her hair, as if there was a one-sentence answer to that question.

Kento knew their type. He'd encountered them all over the world.

As was usual for the breed, they were pretty. In a calculated way. They were both tall and statuesque and wore nylon windbreakers, one bloodred and the other as brash an orange as her lipstick, as if to be properly protected for the weather. But their jackets might have been a child's size, so snugly did they fit against their torsos. Surely there was no shield from the elements when those coverings were worn unzipped so low that Kento could make out the color of each of their bras. Jeans skimmed their long legs down to the spike-heeled boots that looked ready to catch in between the wooden planks of the boat dock.

Both had hair styled to perfection, which was almost pointless if someone was to spend any amount of time outdoors in Seattle. As if to illustrate the point, the mist in the air had turned to rain in the few minutes since they had been chatting, as often happened in the Pacific Northwest. They both wore heavy makeup, and individual raindrops began sticking to their false eyelashes, creating little bubbles.

"Mr. Yamamoto, ready when you are, sir." The yacht's captain appeared with his announcement.

Having just flown in on his private jet from Tokyo, Kento had a couple more legs to his long journey—a boat ride to the Willminson Island harbor and then a limo to the luxury lodge that had been reserved for the destination wedding. He'd spent most of the flight working and was tired, looking forward to a little rest before the numerous events of the extended weekend began to unfold. Plus, he'd learned that once a person was running a multibillion-yen software development empire, there was no such thing as a total escape and he'd be supervising operations from afar over the weekend. So he was ready to board and let the captain set off.

"Ladies, if you'll excuse me. I'll no doubt see you at the welcome reception tonight."

The smiles that had been glued onto their faces both dropped in unison. He didn't know what they were expecting, but their expressions read disappointed. They'd wanted something from him. Just as the rain turned heavy and a downpour began.

Cripes, Kento thought. He couldn't shoo them away and send them teetering in the rain with their heels and wheeled suitcases all the way over to the other dock to take the public ferry. He'd have to give them a ride.

"Come onto my boat. I'll take you," he said, stretching an arm out to help the first one of them onto the deck. They both grabbed hold of him at the same time.

"Thanks, Kento!" one exclaimed and clumsily hoisted herself on. He became part of a tangle of outstretched hands and luggage handles while the rain whipped around, so he didn't notice which of them had thanked him.

"You're a hero," came the other's voice.

"Our knight in shining armor."

It was going to be an endless ride across the Sound if they continued with their sucking-up routines. Did men actually fall for that sort of thing? Not men like him, he affirmed. When just about every human encounter of his formative years had been a verdict on what his financial and social standings were and weren't, Kento had developed a healthy skepticism for people's motivations in wanting to get close to him.

In fact, he'd soon be face-to-face with some of the very people who had ingrained that distrust into him, who'd seared it into him like a hot iron's brand that he still wore like a tattoo. An attitude that he was proud of at this point. While the upcoming weekend was meant to send Lucas and Christy into what would hopefully be a lifetime of wedded bliss, Kento had some less idyllic business of his own to take care of.

After he ushered the two women into the shelter of the boat's cabin, Kento returned to the open air of the stern as it pulled away from the dock. He would no doubt get soaked, but he didn't care. From his vantage point at the back of the yacht, he kept his eyes fixed on the mainland as they pulled away, the sights of the Seattle skyline that he hadn't taken in for years. The Ferris wheel. The renowned food stalls of Pike Place Market. The office skyscrapers. There were the mountains in the distance, dwarfed by Mount Rainier, the tallest in Washington, the stratovolcano that hadn't erupted since the late 1800s.

Kento felt a special nostalgia to once again see the most famous of the city's landmarks, the six-hundred-foot-tall Space Needle observation tower that instantly identified Seattle. As it had since its construction for the 1962 World's Fair, the structure with its flying saucer design watched over the storied city with a parent's caring eye.

Seattle used to be home. It was where he'd grown up and gone to university. After his software design corporation, NIRE, continued to grow and grow, Kento moved his parents to Japan to be with him. His sister now lived in Connecticut, so he no longer had cause to return. Breathing in the wet mist of the Sound, he was reminded that there was nowhere quite like Seattle, the Emerald City, so named for the year-round greenery in and around the metropolis.

It was a city filled with memories for Kento, some good, some not so. In particular, there was one recollection that he needed to bring into the present so that he could put it in the past. A remembrance with dusty blond hair the color of pure sand and eyes so light a brown they were almost transparent. With skin that smelled like sweet cream. The scent that still lingered in his nose, all these years later.

"I hear you and Erin Barclay used to date," MacKenzie blurted after Kento returned to the cabin and instructed the first mate to serve him and his guests a quick coffee for the short journey.

Kento looked her in the eyes but, really, peered right through her. "We did," he answered barely above a whisper. "A long, long time ago."

"And now you're best man and maid of honor at the wedding. That is *so* cute." Amber's voice entered from his side.

"Is it?" Kento raked his fingers through his thick, now soaked hair.

Of course, he'd been honored when his oldest friend asked him to stand beside him as he said his vows to his bride. Especially as the two men no longer saw much of each other. Kento had accepted, though not without trepidation, predicting that Christy would tap her cousin Erin to be the maid of honor. It had been seven years since he'd seen Erin and zero days that he hadn't thought about her. As maid of honor and best man, he knew there'd be expectations that the two would spend a lot of time together, giving speeches, dancing for photographers and fostering a general camaraderie among the wedding party throughout the activities of the weekend.

As he'd thought about it over and over again sitting in his luxury penthouse overlooking kinetic, buzzy Tokyo, Kento began to believe that returning to Seattle for the wedding was perfect for the reckoning that he so desperately needed. Maybe that time spent working closely together would help him finally exorcise Erin from his brain and his soul. Hopefully, he could break free from the hold that his memories still had on him. "Cute." He hypnotically repeated Amber's stupid comment.

"I hope you'll save a dance for me," MacKenzie chirped. "We're bridesmaids, you know."

"Do you want to sit together at the welcome dinner tonight?" Amber asked. Kento found the question annoyingly pushy and didn't respond.

Luckily, neither of them wanted to leave the cabin to go with him to the boat's bow as they neared the island's shoreline. Lush fir trees appeared to cover every inch of earth, tall, full and close together, creating a dense forest. It was an unspoiled and pristine spot that would make for an unforgettable wedding.

Kento felt the tiniest kick of sadness in his gut.

When his boat docked in the harbor, he helped Amber and MacKenzie disembark, refusing their offer that he join them. The public ferry arrived at the same time, delivering other wedding attendees. He recognized a few, scrutinizing the group and looking for that familiar sandy hair but not seeing it.

A covered walkway had been erected to shelter guests from the ferry dock as they loaded into the van that would shuttle them to the lodge. Amber and MacKenzie joined the group. A waiter was there to greet everyone with a tray of champagne in flutes. Continuing to observe the scene from afar, Kento could hear MacKenzie's shrill giggle.

There was a banner hung to welcome their party. It read, Christy and Lucas. Forever Begins Now.

Kento knew that transportation from the harbor to the lodge had been prearranged. But he'd booked his own, guessing that he wouldn't want to be part of the festivities until he'd settled in. He waited for the van full of wedding guests to leave. A second, empty van pulled into position for the arrivals from the next ferry. The waiter set more flutes on his tray and filled them with bubbly.

Only then, in the solitude, did Kento make his way up the gangplank and slip into the black limo that awaited him.

"Did you hear? Harris Denby drained her bank accounts before he vanished."

Erin Barclay entered the lounge adjacent to the lobby of the upscale Locklear Lodge on Willminson Island, where her cousin Christy was marrying longtime boyfriend Lucas. Erin had arrived just in time to overhear a group of wedding guests talking about her.

"Where did his parents finally track him down?"

"Partying in Greece with some European actresses."

"He just left Erin? Without a word?"

She turned away from their view so that she could listen in without yet being spotted.

"What kind of man does that?"

"The kind who lives off his trust fund with nothing expected of him and too much time on his hands. Apparently, his own family's wealth wasn't enough. He went after *Barclay* wealth."

"The passed-down-from-generations, too-much-to-even-count kind of money." A few high-pitched giggles erupted. "Our favorite kind of people."

Bridesmaids and daddy's little rich girls Amber Dutton and MacKenzie VanBurton seemed to know an awful lot about her. They were friends of Christy's that Erin had socialized with a few times over the years. The two stood in a cluster with the three groomsmen, who listened dutifully to the girls as they all sipped something warm-looking from heavy brown mugs.

Was this how the weekend was going to

go? Erin wondered, with gossip swirling about her being freshly dumped by Harris T. Denby III? Who had left her at the town house they'd shared in Spokane, where her parents had created a job for her at one of their offices there. Harris had simply disappeared in the middle of one night. Once he was located and word got out, the media that followed high society jumped on the story and, thereby, made sure that everyone Erin knew had heard about it.

"Christy said she never trusted Harris from the beginning," MacKenzie prattled on.

"Not from the start," Amber echoed.

Erin knew that Christy must have been defending her by telling them that she had never liked Harris. If only she had heeded that warning!

Subtly peering around the lounge, she was still trying to avoid being noticed just yet. The lodge was as rustic glam as she'd remembered when she accompanied Christy and Aunt Olivia to tour it as a possible wedding venue. Everything was done in the finest materials. A fire in the huge stone hearth gave the room a comfortable warmth and smell. Thick rugs covered large areas of the tiled floor. Overstuffed leather furniture and tree-trunk tables were arranged into clusters. Paintings of nature, featuring flora and fauna native to the area, decorated the walls. A buffet table held a selection of coffees and teas as well as small sandwiches, fruit and cookies, all artfully displayed on raised platters.

Erin was hungry. She hadn't eaten since before she left the town house in Spokane to head to the airport for her short flight to Seattle. But she wasn't sure she was ready to face the bridesmaid firing squad and their potential interrogation. As the quintet still had their backs to her, she was able to continue listening for the two words she knew she'd hear. They came immediately.

"You know she used to date Kento Yamamoto?" One of the men spoke the only name that had ever made Erin's heartbeat sputter. Of all the things she was likely to have to face this weekend, seeing Kento again was the scariest.

Amber exclaimed, "We know! He gave us a ride here on his boat."

"On his boat."

"He's a major player in the software sector, isn't he?" another other man in the group asked.

"Major."

"He's *so* gorgeous," MacKenzie threw in.

He was at that. Erin knew that the seven years they'd been apart looked good on him because she'd seen articles in magazines about the young, unmarried billionaire. From the photos she could see that nothing had changed about him being six foot three with hair that was too long for a businessman. Nor the dark, probing eyes and slim hips. Although she'd noticed that his face had matured from that of university student to twenty-eight-year-old CEO.

"And he's megarich," Amber continued to blab.

"Mega."

Kento had brought them to the island on his own boat. Erin wondered how that came about. Unless things had changed, it wasn't like him to go for the gold digger types. In fact, that was what she had always suspected was one of the things that drove him away years ago, this elite Seattle crowd's obsession with money and success. Back then, just like Harris more recently, Kento had disappeared.

She hadn't known why, but he'd vanished just the same, leaving Erin abandoned. Decidedly different was that Harris leaving didn't matter to her all that much. Kento's departure had been another thing entirely. One that, in fact, had altered her life.

As to the bridesmaids, back in the day Kento had loathed people like Amber and MacKenzie, judging men based on their bank accounts or status. Although what would Erin know about Kento's likes and dislikes anymore? She hadn't seen him since he'd gone from a have-not to a most definite have.

"Is he single?"

"Doesn't he live in Japan?"

"Was he born in Seattle?"

"Does he know Harris broke up with Erin?"

"He didn't have a date with him on the boat."

"Is he bringing someone to the wedding?"

"Look him up online."

"Whoosh." One of the guys finally put the kibosh on the gossip. Erin almost let out a chuckle, so laser-focused were these big-haired opportunists. "All I said was that he used to date Erin. I have no further intelligence. Shall we call in the FBI?"

If the two bridesmaids rode across the Sound with Kento, that meant he was already on the property. A pulse dashed through Erin's body at the thought. She glanced behind her as if she might see him suddenly standing right there, eavesdropping on her eavesdropping.

Instead, when she turned around she saw Bettina "Bunny" Marchand Barclay, her mother, coming toward her. Bunny Barclay was probably Seattle's most visible socialite, constantly appearing in the news at a gala fundraiser for a new museum or a mayor's luncheon or the like. Upper crust to a fault, Bunny wore pearls to breakfast. The Barclay fortune belonged to Erin's father, Ingram, the fifth generation of land and property owners who were in possession of a good percentage of Washington state. Her father wouldn't be in attendance for the wedding weekend, as he had important business in Walla Walla.

"You look absolutely gaunt," Bunny trilled as she air-kissed her daughter on each cheek. "I hope there's a makeup artist coming, and immediately."

Erin wasn't aware that she didn't look right. She'd scarcely checked a mirror today.

Since Harris had fled three weeks ago, the days had been a blur spent mostly in the gloomy and overdecorated Spokane town house that she'd never liked, anyway. After Harris's departure, her parents had decided that Erin would move back into their palatial home in Seattle, with the intention of finding her a suitable husband, of course. Because breeding was to be Erin's most important purpose in life. After several disappointments, they'd thought they'd made a perfect match in Harris. How wrong they were. Hair and makeup had been the last thing on Erin's mind lately.

Having already checked into her room, she was certainly planning to shower, dress and groom appropriately for the welcome dinner later that would kick off the wedding festivities. It quickly crossed her mind that she hoped Kento wouldn't be coming down to the lounge now for the afternoon snack, not wanting to see him until after she'd pulled herself together. Not that it should matter, as it was far too late for anything between the two of them. He'd made that abundantly clear when he deserted her without even saying goodbye. Kento, a few others that never developed, then Harris, the aging party boy. Was there anyone on earth who had worse luck with men than she did?

"Erin," Bunny continued, "there are a number of eligible men coming to the wedding I want you to meet."

"It's only been three weeks since Harris left me." Erin sized her mother up like she was crazy. "Isn't a mourning period in order?"

"You do not tell people that Harris *left* you. You say that you found you weren't compatible."

"Mother, do you remember that I mentioned to you a 1902 property in Queen Anne I saw? Now that I'm going to be moving back to Seattle, I'd like to look at buying that for the company."

"You know we have an acquisitions department to handle new purchases. Let's concentrate on finding you a proper match so that the next generation of Barclays is insured."

"That's my purpose in life? I'm just a pedigreed racehorse?"

Erin didn't hide her cynicism. Really, though, what difference did it make? Let her parents choose a mate for her, sure. Her own attempts had ended with love jetting five thousand miles across the Pacific Ocean to build a future that didn't include her.

"And no, at your age we don't waste time licking our wounds."

"Yes, at twenty-eight, I'm an ancient sack of bones."

"The clock is ticking. Let me tell you about someone. Humphrey Colder."

"Kento Yamamoto is here, Mother. Now that he has money, maybe you'd like him better." The words fell out of Erin's mouth before she had a chance to censor herself. He'd devastated her by leaving, but he didn't deserve to be part of a sarcastic joke. Yet she'd always had a suspicion that her parents had had something to do with Kento walking out of her life.

Bunny bristled. Her small mouth pursed. "We deal in traditional wealth, Erin. Established families from the Northwest. Landowners. Not fly-by-night tech billionaires. The Kento Yamamotos of the world aren't our kind of people. They never were and they never will be. Have I made myself clear on that?"

You're not the one who should have been spending your life with him, Erin thought but didn't bother to say, as it was a lost cause.

* * *

Kento surveyed the view from the front porch of the second most deluxe cabin on the Lock-lear Lodge grounds. He'd reserved the largest for Christy and Lucas, his wedding gift to them. His was expansive and constructed in a rich red wood, the porch large enough to house a hammock and a sofa swing. He noted that the enclosed side deck offered complete privacy and was equipped with a sauna, hot tub and outdoor shower. It wistfully occurred to him what a romantic setting this would be for a couple in love.

The vistas were magnificent. Beyond the large stretch of lawn that the cabin opened onto, the dense grove of fir trees so plentiful in the Pacific Northwest stood proud and strong. Their bracing, earthy scent was like no other. It would do Kento some good to take a walk in the forest there, the moist earth under his feet. He couldn't have been farther from his ultramodern office suite in Tokyo.

He heard them before he saw them. Loud voices interrupting the hush of nature. Squishing sounds in the ground.

"Hi, Kento!"

"Hi, Kento! We didn't see you in the lounge."

It was Amber and MacKenzie trotting the footpath that crossed in front of his cabin en route from the lodge's main buildings.

"Hi, Kento." A third voice poked out from between the two. Kento's stomach lunged at the possibility that it might be Erin, whom he hadn't yet seen since he arrived. He'd skipped the revelry at the ferry dock and opted out of the afternoon tea. Was this the moment they'd lay eyes on each other again for the first time this weekend? Would she be happy to see him? He knew what hurt he still carried. What might she?

The clearing between the bridesmaids opened to reveal a short woman with large breasts. She was definitely not Erin. "I'm Divya Nadu, and I've been wanting to meet you." All three of them giggled. Kento wasn't sure if he was disappointed or relieved that he wasn't face-to-face with Erin yet. Although that would be coming soon enough, as everyone was expected at the welcome dinner.

"*Prosperity Magazine* named you one of the top five billionaires under thirty," Divya squealed.

"Did they? What's the criteria for that?"

Kento snickered and folded his arms across his chest. "How did I get into the top five?"

"Oh, good question. I think it was that they predicted your fortunes would continue to grow."

"Based on what?" How familiar this was. All of Kento's life it seemed that within minutes of meeting someone, there was some inquisition as to his positioning and station. He was right to have left this toxicity behind him when he moved to Tokyo after earning his university degree. There were plenty of opportunists there, too, especially as he became more and more successful. But he'd learned how to better detect and fend them off.

It still nagged in his craw, though, how he'd left Erin, the only woman who saw him for who he was not what he had. Clearly she'd wanted him to go. After all, she had participated in his ousting. But he should have said goodbye. What they'd had together was important, and they'd owed each other a final farewell. All these years later and his business with her was still unfinished.

He'd met plenty of women in that time, Ayaka being the only one he'd gotten serious with. Which turned out no better than things did with Erin. The memory of Erin had never left him, though. In a way, it was holding him back. Maybe if he didn't still have foggy dreams of her eyes sparkling in the moonlight, or remember her smiles in the sunshine, he could be free from desiring something he knew he'd never have.

Billionaire bachelor. Ha. Always would be.

"I guess they think your company will get bigger and bigger," Divya continued. "I mean, it's so huge already."

"Huge."

"Enormous."

As these women babbled on, Kento figured it was going to be a long, long weekend.

MacKenzie said, "Let's have a drink at the bar before dinner."

"A little cocktail kickoff."

"And sit with us at dinner, Kento." Hadn't one of them already asked him that earlier? These women didn't know a thing about him other than what they'd read in a magazine. Yet they wanted him to sit with them. Was it any wonder he felt constantly measured?

"Sit with us." Amber was beginning to sound like a pouty little girl. Which, in fact, she was. Divya's smile was as forced and wide as a jack-o'-lantern's. How could he get them to move on?

"If you'll excuse me, ladies," Kento said politely, "I'm going to go inside to get unpacked and dress for dinner. I'll see you there."

"Okay," MacKenzie sang, "but you better at least dance with me."

"Me, too."

"Me, three."

He bowed his head at each of them. Thankfully, they skirted off after a chorus of goodbyes.

Swiping his key card, he stepped into the cabin and took off his shoes. Inside, it was thankfully quiet. The living room contained large furniture that faced the view through the windows. A dining table and chairs could accommodate a private meal for eight should that be desired. The kitchen area was stocked with local brands of gourmet snacks and a basket of fresh fruit. Wines, sodas, waters and a coffee setup stood ready on the counter. A state-of-the-art media center allowed as much connectivity as a guest could want.

The bedroom was furnished with a king-size bed framed by a redwood headboard and posts, made up with plush green plaid bed-ding and a dozen pillows. A small sofa and coffee table faced the wood-burning fireplace as well as a second wall-mounted TV, giving the bedroom options for more than sleeping.

An extravagant bathroom was anchored by a claw-foot bathtub. There was a walk-in shower with glass walls. Shelves held stacks of fluffy towels and baskets of toiletries. Kento unbuttoned his shirt and threw it onto a vanity table. He quickly stripped off all his clothes, ready for a shower to reinvigorate him after a long journey and the grating encounter with the grinning bridesmaids.

Before stepping into the shower, though, he had a change of heart. The weather had cleared and there was even some end-of-the-afternoon sun, so he decided to make use of the outdoor shower.

Knowing the area was fully secluded thanks to its own cluster of trees, he grabbed a couple of towels and strode naked out the door to the side deck. The shower wasn't enclosed in any way. Its wide rain-forest faucet was embedded in a stone wall, leaving everything around it open. He turned the knobs until the spray produced a strong flow. When he stepped under the showerhead, the hot water pouring down onto him in conjunction with the soft breeze across his skin was a sublime combination. He let the water slide down his body, swirling to the drain at his feet. Breathing in, he took his time and allowed the sensations to envelop him. It was truly relaxing.

His nakedness outdoors felt so primal. As if an ancient drum was beating somewhere low within him, marching him toward something unseen. A hunger and virility inside him woke up, breaking out of hibernation. Spreading his arms wide-open like an eagle's wings, he presented his manhood to the blue skies. The water cascaded over his head, down his neck, his shoulders, his chest, his erection. Receiving the downpour, he stood like that, arms outstretched for the longest time. The only thing that kept him from roaring out loud was not knowing how far his voice might carry.

Eventually reaching for the bar of sandalwood-scented soap that had been provided, he began lathering his entire body, scrubbing it into his skin with his hands. Erin was somewhere on the lodge's property, and he'd be seeing her soon. Had she come into his mind so often over the years because she'd wounded him so badly with her betrayal? Was it because he was torn up by regret for running away, never even confronting her about what she'd been part of? Or was it because no woman had ever compared to her and until he saw her again she'd always have a hold on him? That was what he intended to settle this weekend. He'd return to Japan with no more unanswered questions.

In any case, Kento could smell change in the crisp Washington air.

CHAPTER TWO

"No, THE MAID of honor. She's the one Harris Denby dumped."

Erin pretended she didn't hear people talking about her from, literally, behind her back, although she didn't miss a word. She was like a dog that could hear high-pitched sounds that didn't register with humans. It was as if the whole room was talking about her. Again. Her head started to spin. She'd only been on the island for a couple of hours, but it already seemed like a month.

The weekend was full of planned events. Tonight was the welcome dinner. Tomorrow would be the rehearsal and the rehearsal dinner. The day after was the afternoon wedding ceremony, followed by the reception. And the weekend was to conclude with a gift-opening brunch the following morning. Erin didn't know how she was going to make it through with people pointing at her and her mother lining up men for her to meet.

Waiters passed glasses of wine, sparkling water and hors d'oeuvres on trays. There were teeny-tiny apples stuffed with creamy cheese. Cornmeal-fried oysters. Prosciutto-wrapped asparagus. Erin grabbed at everything she could as it was carried past. She hadn't eaten at the afternoon tea once she was commandeered by her mother, who sent her back to her room until her appointment with the makeup artist and hairstylist, deeming Erin unfit for public consumption until then.

The stylist did work wonders, she had to admit. Since Harris had left her, she'd been in a funk and didn't give a hoot about her appearance. So a haircut had indeed been in order, and the nice blowout would look good for the many photos Erin would have to stand for as maid of honor. Her makeup was flattering but not overdone. And the long burgundy, three-quarter-sleeved sheath dress worn with brown lace-up boots seemed spot-on for the evening.

Erin hoped the outfits for each of the weekend's occasions that she and her mother had shopped for conveyed maid of honor status without defying Erin's understated personal style. Unlike the credo that less is more, her mother was always telling her that more is more, that sparkly objects garnered the most attention. But something in Erin's very being had always been repelled by her mother's constant flaunting of their wealth. Something very few people in her life had ever understood. Definitely no one at this wedding, the crème de la crème of Seattle. No one except...

Her eyes inventoried the room with its enormous picture windows showing off the twilight and its bright blue skies over the trees. Erin's scan wasn't to admire the vista outside, though. She was looking for someone inside. A certain tall, dark-haired someone whom she was both desperately dreading and breathlessly excited to see.

"You look absolutely radiant," Erin managed when she hugged her cousin Christy Barclay, soon-to-be Mrs. Lucas Collins. Erin's compliment was a stretch, because she thought the bride was a bit overdone with her ruffled yellow dress. But Erin knew Christy had to be camera-ready the entire weekend.

"Lucas has some great friends I want to introduce you to," Christy whispered in her ear before someone called her away. "Let's get that Harris mess behind you."

First her mother, now Christy! Was every person here determined to either gab about her being ditched or to fix her up with someone? It was embarrassing that everyone in the free world seemed to know about her breakup, and how that was apparently the best topic of conversation they could come up with. Right on cue, Erin's mother approached.

"Thank heavens they gave you a manicure," Bunny quipped, strangely focusing on Erin's nails, which had been polished in a bright violet shade that was similar to her maid of honor gown. Her mother offered another vague insult. "This afternoon you looked like a wild child who climbed out of the Olympic Mountains."

"Thank you, Mother. That's a lovely image."

"Now, where's that Mr. Colder?" Bunny said as she looked for a man different from the one Erin searched to find. "A very interesting prospect for you to talk to."

"After it went so well with Harris," Erin chortled sarcastically, "we know your matchmaking skills are top-notch."

"Don't be rude, Erin. Had you been able to get Harris to settle down, you would have been perfectly stationed for life."

"Oh, I see. It's my fault I wasn't able to turn his cheating, lying ways?"

She knew that she was being snippy when, in reality, she'd all but resigned herself to letting her parents make the match they wanted. One of the arranged Pacific Northwest society marriages that her father insisted made just as much sense now as they had throughout history. Left to her own devices, she'd die a spinster. She'd thought she'd once known what a true union was. What love was. But it stole her heart and flew far away, leaving only a hole that would never be filled.

Fine, she could procreate, carry on the family genes. As long as she didn't have to fall in love. That would be a fate worse than death. The most she could hope for was that she'd end up with someone with whom she'd have some things in common and they could serve their offspring-producing callings with an amiable companionship.

"I forgot something in my room," Erin lied. She followed the waiter with the fried oysters, just needing a break from her mother.

"I've got someone fabulous to introduce you to," Christy sang as she skidded past Erin while she was being led across the room by her husband-to-be. "He coaches basketball with Lucas." The groom was a big and tall man with a ruddy complexion, a high-ranking stockbroker at one of Seattle's top firms. As was his father. As was his father's father. *Old money*, as Bunny loved to point out.

Noticing two couples gesturing to her, Erin was getting dizzy from everyone's attention. The room seemed to be closing in. How could she get everyone to just leave her be?

She was a dutiful daughter. Yet for all of her cynicism about not caring with whom she produced heirs, in the secret, most hidden recesses of her soul, she was screaming for something else. She was starving for adventure. For risk. For passion.

At that exact instant, the moon outside rose and cast a powerful beam down through the window toward the opposite end of the party room. It was white and tapered open like a spotlight positioned on an empty stage. Erin's eyes followed it and she turned in its direction, wondering how moon glow could be streaming so intensely at that one spot and no other. She couldn't see what was over there because too many people were in the way. Without telling them to do so, her feet began moving toward the direction of the light.

The closer she got, the more the clusters of guests moved to the left or to the right, opening a path for her. Her steps became faster. Until she froze when she reached the other side of the room, where a solitary figure stood at the arched entrance to the party. He was observing the scene, almost as if deciding whether to enter. And he was indeed bathed in a moonbeam, or at least that's how it appeared to Erin.

The familiar handsomeness sent shivers racking through her. The high cheekbones, full lips and his imposing height reminding her, as they always had, of drawings of potent Japanese emperors with long swords from centuries gone by. Especially in the shadow profile of the light shining down on him, he commanded all he surveyed. His dark hair still fell in a thick, youthful tousle downward from his forehead, hinting at a rebelliousness despite the fine navy suit perfectly tailored to his lean muscular body.

As if knowing she'd be there, he turned his

head. His gleaming almost-black eyes bored into hers the instant they made contact, causing her breath to shorten, and she went from a casual pose to standing at attention.

Slowly, the seriousness in his face melted to something gentler, where it lingered for a moment. Then the gaze quickly corrected itself, as if the previous move had been a swiftly caught error. He returned to his piercing stare. Kento Yamamoto bowed his head and said only, "It's good to see you again, Erin."

She was a real human. Flesh and blood. Not the almost otherworldly character that inhabited his midnights with snapshot remembrances of hopes long gone. After seven years, more than long enough to shed a skin, Erin Nancy Barclay was in front of him once again. The mixture of emotions Kento felt was like one of those cake beaters that whirled ingredients, wet and dry, salty and sweet, smooth and chewy, until they were too intermingled to separate. He wanted to reach out and hug her in almost equal measure to his desire to turn around and bolt away.

"Did you just get here?" she asked, the

tones of her voice like an old song he hadn't heard in ages.

"A couple of hours ago. I checked in on some work."

"You skipped the welcome tea."

"How was it?"

"I didn't end up staying."

"Why?"

"I got waylaid by my mother."

The corner of his lip tipped up. Some things never changed. "Hmm."

"It's a really long flight for you from Tokyo, isn't it?"

"And oh, yes, we're getting some nice afternoons this time of year."

She looked at him questioningly. "What does that mean?"

"That commenting on banalities is the best we can do after all this time?"

"What would you like to talk about?"

They were off to a rocky start. She was right—he couldn't yet ask what he wanted to. About how she could have participated in the despicable forcing out of him that her parents had enacted. He'd come for those answers, but this wasn't the time or place. Outwardly, they needed to be pleasant exes who were attentive to their best man and maid of honor duties. To lead the bridal party and serve the bride and groom with whatever they needed.

"Did you write your speech?" he asked.

"I drafted out some ideas. Wishing people a happily-ever-after ride into the sunset is a little hard to write when you've just been broken up with."

Broken up with? His jaw locked. He'd heard from Lucas that Erin was living in Spokane with someone and that it was serious. He hadn't talked to Lucas in a couple of weeks other than some emails, in which the groom hadn't mentioned that Erin and her man split up. Kento had assumed that she'd have him in tow for the weekend. He guessed that the boyfriend was certainly someone Erin's parents had sanctioned, as approval was always one of the key tenets in the Barclay family.

Did that mean that she was here on her own for the wedding weekend? Kento's mind began to spin. He'd wanted to see her again, to finally emancipate himself from the shackles their past kept him in. But he needed to do that from a safe distance, with her unavailability serving as an impenetrable barrier that would prevent him from considering things that couldn't be. Erin single and unbound was too risky.

"Someone recently broke up with you?" He decided to play it cool, to pretend like he didn't even know she'd been in a relationship. Meanwhile, at seeing her again, the hurt he'd brought along with him spilled out of his pockets, breathed out of his nose, blinked in his eyes. At the same time, she was so exquisitely beautiful a wail fought to make itself known.

"You mean you haven't heard? It's all anyone seems to be talking about this weekend."

"Did your parents like him?" He couldn't resist the dig. After all, if it weren't for Bunny and Ingram, and Erin's allegiance to the way her parents thought, the two of them might have had a future together. Who knew what could have happened? She could have moved to Japan with him. Or perhaps he wouldn't have gone. They might be married. Have children. For that matter, they could be divorced. There were so many could-have-beens. He wondered if this ex-boyfriend suffered the same fate.

"Indeed. My parents fixed me up with Harris."

Ah, so nothing at all like Kento. "He was the right sort, then?"

Erin blinked a few times. He realized he was being cruel. After not seeing her for so long, his emotions had had a chance to compound. He needed to take it slow. Watch what he said. She'd just been broken up with. Even though he didn't know the circumstances, he was never one to kick someone when they were down. In spite of how many times that had been done to him.

"He looked great on paper, as they say. In reality, it didn't work out that way."

"I'm sorry to hear that." Was he? Whether or not she was with someone should have no effect on him.

"It's another cliché, but better to find out sooner rather than later."

She didn't look exactly the same as she did in the mental photo album he flipped through far too often. From a ponytailed girl with designer jeans and purses, her wealth something that had always been visible, she'd ripened into a striking woman who wore her wine-colored dress with style. The close fit outlined her slim body, the one he'd known every inch of in days gone by. His belly tightened at the recollection.

Her eyes were a little drawn, perhaps revealing her recent romantic failure. He found himself wondering about the details, why he'd broken up with her. But those unusually light brown eyes of hers were still her most arresting feature. He remembered peering into them for hours on end, trying to count the little gold flecks in her irises. He was glad that tonight her lips were covered in only a natural-looking gloss. It was easier that way to imagine…

They stood contemplating each other, perhaps melting into the same remembrances, perhaps opposite ones. Kento's body was so alert and on edge that he wondered if his nerve endings could take much more. He felt almost out of control, something he wasn't accustomed to.

"What about you?" Fortunately, Erin recircuited his brain. "Single, married, divorced, gay?"

"Married," he tittered. Did something register in those eyes of hers in response to his answer? "To a billion-yen software development company." Then, did he sense her relief after his explanation?

"I've heard. So, after graduation when you left…to work with your uncle in Tokyo, you never came back?"

"At first I'd come to see my parents now and then." He'd never attempted to see Erin on those trips. Her parents had made their lack of welcome infinitely clear. And she'd proved that she wasn't capable of defying them. "I moved them to Japan a couple of years ago, and I haven't been back here since."

Kento's parents. Who couldn't be more different from Erin's. Who didn't have money in the bank but labored so hard to pay for their two children to go to good schools and top universities. Because they wanted them to have options. His sister had become a lawyer. And Kento had found his niche in software.

Ultimately, what his parents wished for him proved to be a double-edged blade. The exclusive schools with the high academic reputations certainly taught him well. But being the charity case among the upper crust, one of the few who had to apply for every scholarship and dollar of financial assistance available, set him up for constant embarrassment and ridicule. Rich kids showed no mercy for the übersmart boy who received help with his tuition. Kento bore those scars silently for his parents, though, who were so proud of every good exam score and achievement of their son's.

"How are they?" She'd only met them a few times, as they were always busy working at their small grocery store in the nearby city of Tacoma.

"I was so glad when I could give them the word a couple of years ago that they should retire because I could easily provide for them. Typical for them, they were too modest to let me buy them a spacious home. Instead, they chose an apartment in a retirement living community just big enough to suit their needs." Unlike Erin's parents, who wore their wealth on their sleeves, their cars and their mansions. And, most especially, with the people they surrounded themselves with, whom they picked and chose as if selecting only the shiniest unbruised apples from the farmer's basket.

"Kento, Erin, will you kick off the evening with an impromptu toast?" Lucas yelled over to them from the gaggle he was standing with. The reminder of the reason they were there startled them both, with Kento lost in days past.

"I guess it's showtime." Kento shrugged. He gestured with an outstretched arm that they should enter the thick of the group.

After doing so, when they were surrounded by partygoers, a waiter appeared with a microphone. Erin took it and began. "It's great to see everybody here. On behalf of Christy and Lucas and their parents, welcome to Locklear Lodge."

Kento reached to tip the mic toward him, noting the tingly contact his fingers made with Erin's. "Or to be known this weekend as the Forever Begins Now Inn," he said, repeating the sentiment printed on the banner that had greeted guests getting off the ferry earlier. "We wish you all the health and joy in the world."

"And children," a male voice in the crowd added.

"And money," another yelled, earning a laugh from everyone.

Erin finished with, "Let's enjoy our dinner as we begin to celebrate the nuptials of these two very special people."

Fortunately, that appeared to be sufficient for the moment, because people clapped and then began making their way to the dining area of long tables set up with a campfire theme.

The best man and maid of honor presided over the guests as they took seats.

"Kento!"

"Kento!"

"Kento!"

The three voices he'd already come to know charged toward him like a battle army. He caught Erin mashing her lips together as if to stifle a laugh.

"Hi, Erin."

"Hi, MacKenzie, Amber and Divya," she answered.

Ah, so she knew the three barracudas.

"Kento, we're sitting together, aren't we? You promised!"

"You did!"

He'd done nothing of the kind and might rather starve than have to endure dinner conversation that would no doubt pertain to his holdings in the Tokyo Stock Exchange.

Thinking quickly to help him out, Erin

broke in with, "I'm sorry. We're obligated to sit with the bride and groom."

The three mouths that again wore the most unfortunate bright shades of lipstick drooped into mopes.

"Okay…" Divya whined. "But you'd better at least dance with us this weekend."

"Yeah."

"Yeah."

With that, the three clip-clopped away on their high heels.

Kento could have almost kissed Erin for getting him out of their clutches. Absolutely almost kissed her.

"Oh. Kento. Yes, hmm…how nice to see you again." Erin's mother was one of the last to enter the party. Bunny stumbled over her words. "I hear your company is doing fabulously."

"Mrs. Barclay." Kento bowed his head, the Japanese custom that must be second nature to him now. Without warmth or familiarity, he moved no closer to Erin's mother than where he was standing. He certainly wasn't going to give her a hug. Bunny and Ingram had made no attempt to hide their disapproval of him back when he and Erin were dating, and there was no reason to think they would warm up to each other now. It was far too late for that.

It hadn't been of interest to her parents that Erin was her happiest when she was with Kento. They'd had a connection unlike anything she'd ever known. When they were alone together, the outside world disappeared. Her family's wealth and his family's lack of it meant nothing. What was important was smiling into each other's eyes and the passionate kisses that fortified her like nutrition. Looking back, she knew it was a cocoon they'd existed in, university students excited to exchange ideas, share insights, make love. With him, she was alive. Inspired. Involved.

"I think you're sitting over there." Erin pointed to a few of Bunny's contemporaries in an effort to get her away from Kento as quickly as possible. Her mother seized the opportunity and immediately joined her friends.

They made their way to the long, narrow table, where they sat opposite each other. Set chuck wagon—style in keeping with the woodsy lodge, it was a chic and expensive fantasy of roughing it, of course. Sterling silver utensils were styled flat and plain, looking like they were meant for campfire eating. The dinner plates were also metal, and the water glasses were short and solid. Colorful bandannas served as napkins at each setting. Instead of floral centerpieces, groupings of small logs and pine cones were stacked as if they were ready to be kindled.

Erin took her seat with her uncle, the father of the bride, Vernon, to her left and Christy on her right. On the other side of the table, Kento was seated between the bride's and groom's mothers. Servers brought baskets of warm sourdough bread and pots of soft butter wrapped in more bandannas. Private reserve wine was poured into tin cups as the first course, cioppino, was served in bowls with handles, continuing the homespun theme. The tomato broth was deep red, and the stew was packed with plump shellfish. Erin spooned a bite into her mouth. A guitar player in the corner of the room strummed country songs.

"Kento sure looks good after all this time," Christy whispered in Erin's ear. "Is he seeing anyone in Japan?"

"I have no idea," Erin said in return, even

though she thought whispering in each other's ears was rather childish.

"I told you," Christy continued, "you should talk to Demarcus Hall, sitting next to Amber." She gestured with her head as if Erin wouldn't know where to look otherwise. Erin had recognized him as one of the group listening to the giggle girls' gossip earlier at the afternoon tea. She'd certainly noticed that Demarcus was a nice-looking man in a tan suit politely listening to Amber, whose mouth never stopped moving.

Sure that Kento wouldn't have heard the exchange between her and Christy, her eyes nonetheless darted across the table, over the mini log centerpiece, to check on him as he chatted with Lucas's mother. His eyes shot briefly to her and then back to his conversation.

It was nothing less than surreal to be in his presence again. His invisible pull was so powerful it was as if there was only an inch between them rather than a table. As if she could feel his breath on her. No wonder that a few minutes ago it had seemed to her that the moon was shining down on him. The moon existed only for him.

She sneaked another peek while he was bringing a spoonful of stew to his mouth, reacquainting herself with his big hands and their long fingers. She could almost sense them on her skin as if it was yesterday, not years, since they'd last touched her. The cioppino had no idea how lucky it was to be crossing his lips.

Erin herself was almost too nervous to eat, though she nibbled small spoonfuls for the activity it provided. How different this moment would have been if Harris had waited until after the wedding to desert her. With his extroverted personality, he would have sucked up all of the oxygen in the room and demanded her full attention. Not leaving her alone like this, inside her mind, to reminisce about Kento and days long ago.

On a day shortly after their university graduation, they were to meet at their favorite bakery café in the city's Belltown neighborhood. The day before, Kento had been with her at her parents' house, and when Erin was coming back into the room after a phone call, she'd observed something suspicious. Her parents were in a heated discussion with him. He kept snapping his head back at what they were saying, as if he was surprised by it, almost as if they were delivering blows. His body had been taut with tension. All Erin had been able to catch when she reentered the room was her father saying to him, "Just so we understand each other."

She'd been looking forward to the coffee date so that she could ask him about the conversation. Especially as, when she asked them, her parents had denied that anything strange occurred. Kento would provide the truth. Arriving at the bakery ahead of him, Erin ordered a tea latte and a dill-and-goat-cheese scone.

Little did she know when she snagged the window table to look out on a rainy afternoon that she'd be sitting there alone until after dark. Picking at the scone and bitty sips of her latte ended up as a clean plate and empty cup. After Kento was past a reasonable amount of late, phone calls to inquire went straight to his voice mailbox. Finally, Erin acknowledged that he wasn't coming, and she left.

Could something have happened to him, she fretted? He could have been lying in a hospital somewhere, or worse. After a horrific night of worry, it wasn't until the next day that she was finally able to reach his roommate and hear the news that Kento had boarded a flight for Tokyo. Taking the offer of a job from his uncle Riku that Erin had thought he was going to turn down. She must have read the situation between them very wrongly indeed.

The welcome dinner progressed with Erin and Kento stealing glances at each other over their plates of cowboy pepper steak, jacket potatoes and sautéed green beans. Bunny sauntered by and whispered in Erin's ear for her to sit up straight as, unforgivably, she must have been slouching. "Eleven o'clock." Bunny did one of her nonobvious-obvious finger points. "Jack Piccadilly. Accounting firm in Pioneer Square, keeps the books on everyone who's anyone in Seattle finance."

"Is he the one with the three hairs on his head doing a comb-over?" Had all of Seattle's best sons under thirty been taken, and now Bunny was looking within the available crop of *older* gentlemen?

"We're going to find you an appropriate match, Erin. Weddings are a wonderful place to get things started."

Kento made Lucas's mother smile with

something he said. She dropped her bandanna napkin, and he instantly reached down to the floor to retrieve it for her. She smiled in recognition like a schoolgirl. Bunny's voice sounded like an insect in Erin's ear that she swatted away. Thankfully, her mother moved on.

She stood up, telling Christy, "Excuse me." Out of the corner of her eye, she could see Kento watching her go.

Working her way through the narrow channel between the tables, she overheard someone she didn't know say to their dinner companion, "That's the one Harris Denby dropped like a hot potato."

Glancing behind her, she saw MacKenzie, Amber and Divya had wasted no time in surrounding Kento after Erin left the table. Not to mention a few other overtly flirty women. The look on his face told her that they all grated on his nerves. She hadn't known whether he was with someone or was going to bring a date to the wedding. Even if his money wasn't good enough for Ingram and Bunny, the sheer volume of it was attractive to the bounty hunters. It seemed as if the both of them were going to be driven crazy this weekend by matchmakers, gossipers and hangers-on. If only there was a way to get everyone off their backs!

Instead of going to the ladies' room, Erin darted through the lobby and out the lodge's front doors. The sky was pitch-black and a constellation of stars filled the sky.

The evening air was nippy, and she hadn't brought along a sweater or wrap. But as she moved farther and farther away from the lodge, the darkness and quiet were welcoming. She continued into the night, reassuring herself she'd get through this. Although if one more person made reference to Harris leaving her, she thought she might blow a fuse.

Honestly, she also need to process seeing Kento again. Unlike Harris's flashy personality, Kento's magnetism was grounded and solid, like one of the majestic trees in front of her, with unseen roots and a firm standing on the earth. No one else had ever reached down right into her soul like he had.

A cold breeze swept under her dress and chilled her to the bone. She wrapped her arms around herself as she shivered. Behind her, she heard a rustling and figured the wind was kicking up. The night was wild, untamed, making her wish she could emulate it. But it was time to go back inside and be civilized for dessert. She'd make an effort to get to know some of the guests she'd never met and smile for every photo.

As she was about to turn around and go back, she heard leaves crunching again. Suddenly, she felt a presence behind her. Her body startled as a low voice hummed into her ear, "Are you cold?" just as Kento put his suit jacket around her shoulders. It felt like a long-lost blanket that she had been searching for everywhere. She pulled it tightly around her. Involuntarily, her cheek rubbed itself against it, and she inhaled its scent. Kento's scent. "The stars are beautiful, aren't they?"

CHAPTER THREE

"WHAT ARE YOU doing out here?" Erin turned around to face Kento after he'd slipped his jacket around her slender shoulders in an impulse that managed to feel affectionately familiar and crackling new at the same time. With the moon and stars above them, Erin was luminous. A harsh intake of the night air barely hid his reaction.

"Same as you, I'd imagine. I could use a break from the crowd." It was true that Kento had been looking for a reason to get out of the party room. Besides the bridesmaids, it seemed like every unmarried woman on the island for the wedding had been trying to make his acquaintance. The wealthy class of the Northwest was an insular bunch. A person practically had to have made their money during the Klondike Gold Rush to be legitimate in their books.

Now that Kento had amassed a fortune, his new *foreign money*, as some of them regarded it, was apparently good enough for some of them to try to get near, even if it wasn't respected. And so the women here were marching their cosmetically altered assets in a parade for him. It was no different in Japan—prospectors came in every race, creed and color. He had bitter memories from Tokyo as well, though not as many.

He supposed there were men who would take advantage of the situation. They wouldn't care about ultcrior motives when receiving attention from these glittery objects. Kento understood. These women used their wiles as currency. Everything was a bargaining chip. A commodity. Everything had its price. Erin's family thought quite literally in that way.

As if money and accomplishment were the only ways to define a person. He'd never encountered anyone who really saw him. Not growing up poor here and not staggeringly wealthy in Japan. Not Ayaka. He'd originally thought that Erin was the exception to the rule. That he'd found his soul mate. Until he learned the hard, burning way that he'd been very wrong. Erin was, and always would be, an heiress to not only a financial portfolio but to a way of thinking.

Still, watching her hold the lapels of his jacket around her after all this time stirred him inside. *His* jacket. Once he'd gotten over the squeeze to the gut from seeing her after so long, he was grateful. He required this. To be with her here in the States, no longer the ghostly mystery still haunting him from across a gigantic ocean.

"We have to be *on* this weekend," she said. "How are we going to survive it?"

"I was expecting you to be huddled with your boyfriend when I saw you again." A boyfriend whose jacket she'd already have over her shoulders, signaling that Kento's was unwanted and that she belonged to someone else.

"So was I."

"What went awry?"

"My parents."

"What do you mean? I thought you told me they liked him." Kento didn't allow his smirk to grow wide. The conversation never veered far from Bunny and Ingram.

"They chose him for me. A founding family in the Pacific Northwest—they own fleets of cargo ships and whatnot. Could have been a great merging of families."

"Right, that sounds like a business transaction that would make your parents ecstatic." The sarcasm poured off his tongue. Her eyes looked glassy in the moonlight, almost as if she was going to cry. He hadn't meant to upset her with his tone. Even though she was at the top of the list of people who had instilled the cynicism he lugged like a ball and chain.

"What my parents hadn't spent any time on was figuring out if Harris and I were compatible past our family coffers. You have to at least like a person a little bit, even if it was an arranged union, don't you?"

"I wouldn't know." More quips in his voice.

"If my parents had investigated a little better, they'd have heard the common knowledge—he was a cliché bon vivant with the yachts and the models in bikinis and all of that bling. He had no interest in settling down in Spokane, or anywhere else. Or with me."

"You found out after you were already together?"

"I was willing to give it a try. I'm not expecting to find love after..." Her voice trailed off, making Kento wonder what she wasn't saying. "But they could at least try to find me someone who actually wants to be in a relationship."

Kento snickered. Which finally made a small smile appear on Erin's face. That was part of what had made them work as a couple, their ability to laugh even when the going was at its toughest. He was glad to bring her some relief from what was obviously a painful recollection. "So what happened?"

"We dated for a while, attending charity functions and the like, as good heirs do, and then our parents pushed us to move in together. We played at the domestic routine. Within a month Harris began disappearing, first for long weekends and then for weeks at a time."

"Where did he go?" Even though Kento was bitter about what had happened between them, he wouldn't have wished her the disappointment or shame she was describing. After all, he had left her, too. He hated that he'd hurt her, that he'd never said goodbye. In fact, the guilt of that decision tortured him still. To hear that another man had left her without an explanation tore at his heart.

Forces opposed within him. On one hand he'd never forgive her for being complicit in her family's doings against him. Yet on the more mature other, he felt sorry for her inability to break away from their hold. He respected family loyalty, so he couldn't blame her. It just made no sense that this beautiful and dynamic woman wasn't making her own decisions.

"Martha's Vineyard. Rome. Rio. You name it. When I asked Harris if I could go with him, he'd say it was for business and that there was no place for me there."

"You knew he was lying?"

"He had no business to take care of. And even if I didn't know he was lying at first, it wasn't long before my gossipy so-called friends—" she gestured her head toward the lodge, where the snooty party guests were probably forking into their desserts "—sent me photos and videos they saw online. Harris was either too uncaring or too stupid to even try to keep his image clean for his parents' sake, let alone mine."

"I hate the internet."

Erin belly-laughed at his joke, as obviously his multibillion-yen business was dependent on the high-tech world. She was so infectious that he laughed, too, until the sound of their laughter permeated the silent darkness that surrounded them.

She had wounded him deeply, the most profound cut he'd ever received, a knife stab that would impair his breathing for the rest of his life. Yet he felt relief to be near her again. Finally. She'd never know the torment she had caused him. The replaying in his mind of the times they shared. They were only together for a year, but it shaped him. She didn't assess him, unlike everyone else. He could just *be* around her, relaxed, with nothing to prove. He'd learned who he was through her.

Their coupling was unlikely, the well-to-do white girl and the son of a Japanese grocery store owner. Yet they created something genuine together. They were natural around each other, just as their laughter was now. It was as if they were the only one in the other's life who saw through to their insides, laying their souls bare. They'd met in the early fall of a university class and by graduation had dreamed of a future together. She spent more time in the cramped apartment he shared with a roommate than she did in the mansion where she grew up. Until Ingram and Bunny squelched everything.

The recollections of those days and nights together still called out to him, randomly in the middle of a conference or looking at a flower. Confusing his conviction that avoiding relationships altogether was the solution. He'd never met, or believed he'd ever meet, anyone like Erin. He'd never experienced that closeness with Ayaka or anyone else he'd dated. He'd been given one chance at the real thing, or at least he'd thought he had, before Erin and her family snatched the dream away from him. That was the result of taking a chance on trust, of opening his heart. That's why he so desperately wanted to see Erin one last time, to liberate himself from the hold she had on him.

Because although he'd never love again, he did need some companionship and fun. As he approached thirty, the lone-wolf life was unsatisfying. He had sexual encounters with women here and there, after which he couldn't get away fast enough. Even that was growing tiresome. He knew he'd never genuinely partner again, but maybe some kind of casual understanding with a woman was possible. After Erin and then Ayaka, he'd closed himself off. It wasn't healthy. Except how could he hope to have anything when he compared every woman to Erin and found them lacking? He had to find a way this weekend to let go of her once and for all.

"This is good," Erin said as she pulled his jacket to her tighter in a way that made him feel like his arms were wrapping around her instead of the garment. "A moment's tranquility from being fed to the sharks."

"I know what you mean."

"Our wedding party jobs will keep us busy, although they haven't stopped me from being the most gossiped-about maid of honor in Washington State history. And everyone has someone new for me to meet."

"A destination wedding without a date. The pressure is already killing me. Get me back to Japan." They laughed again. Kento had been working especially hard lately to launch a new accounting software program. It was a huge hit in the marketplace, his biggest yet, and the stress had left him drained. Howling into the star-filled Seattle sky with Erin Barclay was about the best remedy he could possibly imagine.

"Actually, I was thinking something kind of outrageous," she said.

"I already like the sound of that."

"If I was here at the wedding with a date, that would show everyone that I'm not just Harris Denby's old castoff. And get the matchmakers and my mother off my back at least for the weekend."

"So you're going to call someone and ask them to come to the island?"

"Oh, no, I wouldn't have anyone to call." He was surprised that she said that so matter-of-factly. She must know dozens of men who would jump at the chance to be with her, even without her family's name. "No one I could trust, anyway. It was just a crazy thought."

With the moon and stars as their only light, Kento could make out Erin's outline as they walked the outskirts of the lodge's property, beyond the courtesy lamps stationed to keep guests on their path. The two of them alone together again at last. Unexpectedly, he pulsed with the urge to pull Erin from the perimeter into the tempestuous unknown of the adjacent forest. He could imagine pinning her up against one of the enormous tree trunks, pressing his body against hers, into hers, as he took her lips without restraint. He could only shake his head in amazement of his own thoughts.

"These people are your family and friends, yet you want to pretend to be romantically involved with someone even though you're not?"

"I just want a break from being talked about, you know?"

"Oh, do I. Don't forget I've been a great source of amusement and ridicule for your crowd ever since I was a kid."

"Look, Kento has the same ratty backpack as he did last year."

"Maybe we should all chip in and buy him a new one."

"Can you believe no one picks him up from school? He takes the bus."

"The bus? Ew."

He'd had to endure the teases and taunts. As a boy, he wasn't invited to the extravagant birthday parties with the clowns and the pony rides. When he was a young teen, pretty girls snubbed their pert noses at him in the school hallways.

"That wasn't my crowd, as you say," Erin defended herself. "That was my family's."

"In any case, I was thrown into the center of it."

"Did you ever tell your parents what you went through?"

"No, of course not. It was out of the love my parents had for my sister and me that they insisted we go to the best private schools in Seattle. We'd sit at our kitchen table, the four of us, year after year filling out the financial assistance and scholarship forms that could make it possible."

"I remember your parents as very kind."

"I did everything I could to help them. I studied hard to excel in my academic subjects. Played sports and the violin. Volunteered my time at hospitals and interned at tech companies. Everything I could to be a desirable candidate for whatever tuition aid we could apply for."

"I don't think back then I really considered just how different our home lives were. We'd kind of created our own little world, you and me, right?"

Yes, they had been more an oasis for each other than they'd ever realized.

"In one respect, it all paid off. I graduated high school with many honors and received acceptance at high-ranking universities. You know at Rainier U, I was invited into prestigious fraternities and social clubs."

"I remember you said you never felt truly welcomed."

"The positive outcome of all of that negativity was that I got tough and worked even harder."

"If it's any consolation, when I was with you was the first time I'd ever really chosen the company I kept. I'd never connected with anyone like we did."

Her words echoed in his chest. Perhaps she was saying something he'd always wanted to hear. Although her lament didn't make him forget what had happened between them. Kento was not a person who was capable of forgetting. Indeed, it was remembering that drove him. Motivated him. And it would continue to do so.

"That wasn't enough for you to stand up to your parents, though, was it? Instead, you stayed behind their shield." There. He'd said it.

"What are you talking about? You're the one who left. Without even a word."

Kento hadn't meant to get into a rehash of

the past. He supposed he was just incapable of bull. Her saying that when she was with him was the only time she'd chosen her own companion had sent fire up his spine.

There was nothing to reconsider. Or process. His intention was merely to see Erin again, to be near her, so that his soul and mind could say a formal goodbye. Her non-place in his life was like a sickness. All he wanted was the cure.

What are you talking about? You're the one who left. Indeed he was, but she knew why.

Kento had a strange niggling. Was it possible that he remembered things differently than what had actually transpired? Digging into historic record wasn't what he'd come to do, yet it itched like a bug bite begging to be scratched.

He turned his head toward her, the moonlight glistening off her hair like her locks held tiny sparkles that only he could see. He'd forgotten many things about her. Like her exact height, which he could see was perfect to lay her head against his shoulder. He'd forgotten those graceful fingers that now held his jacket around her shoulders. The fingers that she'd thread through his when they walked down the street. Bags too heavy with books and electronics, sometimes he'd show off for her by carrying both of theirs. More glorious than he remembered were her pillowy lips, which under the stars looked especially ripe for the claiming. If there was any chance of him surviving the weekend, he'd have to get thoughts like kissing her against a tree out of his mind.

When the funky beat of a popular song crashed sound into the hush of their walk, they realized they'd been outside for a long time.

"Deejay," they said in unison.

"We'd better go back in."

Several heads turned when Kento and Erin returned to the welcome dinner together. If she'd thought of it, she'd have gone to the ladies' room to stall so that Kento could have walked in alone with her arriving a few minutes later. As it was, she felt the scrutiny of many eyeballs. One thing she did know was that when he flattened his palm against her back as he guided her back to the party, she had to fight to keep her facial expression neutral because her body sizzled from head to toe.

Darn him for being able to cause that response in her after all this time! Outside, in the dark, when he'd startled her by coming up from behind and placing his jacket around her shoulders, her body's sense memory instantly took her back. How much she'd always craved his touch when they were together. After they'd part to go to classes or some other business, she couldn't wait to get back into his arms. His close embrace became quite simply her favorite place to be. He'd always held her tightly, possessively. Even at twenty-one he was sure and solid, a take-charge person who had the fortitude to persevere no matter the obstacles. She hadn't envisioned his future career at the time, but creating and helming a massive corporation was not hard to picture, even then.

"How dare you make me miss dessert," he joshed. He was right; waiters were already clearing the empty dessert plates. The remnants of a milk chocolate tart with salted caramel sauce looked delicious.

"Hey, you came outside on your own volition. I just happened to be out there," she shot back to him with a smile.

"You ensnared me with your shivering

shoulders. What kind of best man would I be if I didn't give you my jacket?" Although she'd returned said jacket to him once they got back inside, Erin could still sense it on her, around her, as distinctly his. Intoxicating.

"Can you forgive my shoulders?"

"I'll consider it. If they get me cake."

Bridesmaid Divya, who was jumping up and down for no explainable reason while waving frantically at Kento, called out, "When's my dance?"

He leaned to get very close to Erin's ear, so near that she could feel the warm stream of his exhale as he whispered ever so lightly, "Cake."

His voice coated her, sweet and thick as the caramel sauce. Not missing a beat, as a waiter walked by with an untouched slice of the tart on a plate, Erin relieved him of it and handed it to Kento.

"That's my girl" was his response. Erin's jaw dropped at his word choice as she watched Divya continue to bounce up and down like she was on a spring.

His girl.

She was his girl. Until she wasn't. Five thousand miles away kind of wasn't. She could never forget the desertion. Especially when he'd never explained why he went. Outside, he'd made reference to her hiding behind her parents, but he hadn't explained specifically what he meant.

"Can I get a shot of you two?" the photographer, Billy, gestured to bring Erin and Kento together for a photo. As he posed them, Kento took hearty bites from his tart, making *mmm* sounds that were ridiculously sexy. Once they were in position, Erin took the plate from him, which was met with a frown that made her grin.

"Do I have cake on my face?"

She inspected the area around his exquisite, sensual mouth. Had there been even the slightest crumb, she would have had the opportunity to brush it away with her fingers, an activity that sounded delightful. She'd almost melted into liquid when he'd merely wrapped his jacket around her.

Billy requested, "Look at me, please." The best man and maid of honor conceded and smiled their brightest and best. The photographer shifted them again for the shot he wanted. He then brought over Lucas and Christy for some photos of the foursome.

When they were done, Lucas took Erin's hand and said, "May I dance with the maid of honor?" As she accompanied the groom to the dance floor, she saw the three bridesmaids lunge toward Kento. Fortunately, he quickly took Christy's hand to follow Lucas's lead. The four of them began to dance to an upbeat song. At the deejay's urging, other guests joined.

"Dumped her like a sack of laundry from what I was told. Sent her running right back to Mommy and Daddy Barclay."

Erin overheard a couple dancing near them and could hardly believe the glee in their voices at her misfortune. Kento heard it, too, and shot them a scowl. This was why she had come up with the pretend-boyfriend idea. If people were going to gossip, let them marvel at how fast she'd found another man so soon after her breakup rather than continue to make fun of her about Harris.

A romantic ballad began. Lucas brought Erin a respectable distance to him and they began their dance. Within a verse or two, though, the photographer appeared and wanted to do some shots of the bride and groom dancing together. That left Erin and

Kento standing on the dance floor. He raised his palms up in surrender as if there was only one option.

With a cute bow from the waist, he asked, "May I?" Not waiting for an answer, he swept his arm around her waist and pulled her to him.

Her body met his, a divine joining from a muddled dream she'd had so many years ago. Docile, she got lost in his muscular chest, his shoulder span so broad and arms so long she felt completely enveloped. It was almost as if in his embrace she could finally breathe again. Being so close together, as their maid of honor and best man roles were going to necessitate, she'd need to gird herself against his allure, to remember that moments like this were fake. He'd already broken her heart once before, and he would be jetting off forever in just a few days.

After they'd danced a little, she replayed the conversation they'd had outside. She tilted her head back to ask him, "What did you mean before when you said that I stayed behind my parents' shield?"

"When your parents decided that the way

to get me out of the picture was by making it worth my while, you went along with it."

"Get you out of the picture? Worth your while? You're the one who left for Tokyo without a trace."

"I was angry. And frightened. I think my feelings were justified. There was nothing to say."

"You were angry about what?" She was getting tired of this cryptic conversation. Here she was in Kento Yamamoto's arms after seven long years, and he was making references to things she didn't understand. She glanced away from him and spotted her mother at the edge of the dance floor. Erin noticed how rigidly her teeth were clenched. Her fists were balled. Even though it was perfectly legitimate for the two of them to be dancing together, Bunny was absolutely livid at the sight.

"We can be honest at this point, Erin." He brought her attention back as he swayed them in dance. "I know you knew about it. They told me they had discussed it with you and that you were in agreement it was for the best. It made sense. Your parents' social stratum has entrance criteria that I was never going to meet. They were right."

"What are you talking about?" What on earth had happened that day before he'd stood her up at the bakery? Despite repeated questioning, her parents had denied that anything unusual had transpired, so she never got any further insight into what happened.

Just so we understand each other.

She'd only heard the last of it, what her father said. What had there been to *understand*? Her parents probably assumed she and Kento would separate after graduation. He wasn't *their kind*, as they always categorized people. They were going to uphold their moneyed little Seattle orbit. But Kento was ambitious and hardworking, and she'd hoped her parents respected that she cared for him. She had been sure that *he* at least had *known* that she did.

"You walked in on the conversation. And must have known what it was about. You certainly didn't ask any searching questions about it."

"You never gave me the chance," Erin snapped back. Although nagging in the back of her mind, suddenly, was the same question.

Why *hadn't* she asked more questions? Tried harder to get to the truth? "I do remember that when I came back into the room, you were rigid and eager to leave. The air was thick enough to cut with a knife."

She'd sensed that something was wrong. Kento had always had little patience for her parents and she rarely left him alone with them, so it wouldn't have been surprising if they'd said something that offended him. They'd probably made some kind of elitist statement that went against his grain. She hadn't read that much into his bad mood at the time. Just as she'd decided not to be concerned that the kiss he gave her at the door wasn't his typical, full of decisiveness and heat. It was distant, perfunctory, impersonal. She didn't know it then, but it wasn't a goodnight kiss—it was a goodbye.

"Afterward," she continued her account, "I asked my parents what you three had been talking about, but I never got a direct answer."

"So you let it go at that. You didn't fight for me."

"I didn't know I needed to. You never explained, either."

"They told me you knew."

While they continued to dance and hold up appearances, both were becoming palpably upset.

"Knew what, Kento?"

"About your parents' proposition."

"Huh?"

"They wanted to make sure I fully comprehended that I was just a college fling for you. Now that we'd graduated, you'd be beginning your adult life, and that didn't include me. To make sure I got the point, they offered me a very large sum of money to go away and never contact you again."

"They did what?"

"You heard me." Erin's eyes opened wide. Her heart pounded a thousand beats a minute. Snippets of that day flooded her brain. What her parents had told her was not the truth.

"They twisted it all around to make you look like the bad guy," she eked out in a constricted voice. "When I found out you'd left, they had a *told you so* attitude." Saying that he was just the sort to flee without an explanation. Exactly the person they worried he'd be. They'd lied to their dumb, trusting daughter. And they must have told different lies to him.

Offered him money! And told him she was in agreement about it! Erin was sickened at what her parents had done. She glared back to where her mother had been standing, but Bunny was no longer there. Erin's head spun like a top. Her arms fell from around Kento's neck. She had to get away again, couldn't stand being in the fishbowl of the dance floor. She needed to be alone to absorb the shocking news he had just delivered. "I need to go to my room," she muttered and bolted off, leaving him standing alone. Behind her she heard three loud voices rise above the music.

"Kento!"

"Kento!"

"Kento!"

CHAPTER FOUR

"GOOD MORNING." KENTO waved when he saw Erin walking toward him in the lodge's lobby the next morning.

"Good morning." Erin shot back a wan, tired smile. "I got your message. You're right, we do need to talk."

With a few hours until their wedding party duties began for the day, he'd hired a car to pick them up to take them to island's harbor, where he'd arranged to have a boat waiting for them.

In her jeans, athletic shoes and waterproof jacket, she was dressed appropriately for the boat ride. Last night she'd been an elegant maid of honor in that burgundy-colored dress. She was just as pretty in her casual gear. He hadn't forgotten how lovely her face was in the early-morning light, yet it was even more striking than he had remembered. Her skin looked as smooth as velvet, and although those translucent eyes hadn't had enough sleep, they were still mesmerizing in their honeyed, crystalline uniqueness.

"Are you ready?"

She nodded.

After the car ride to the harbor, he helped her onto the boat. Once they made their way into the cabin, the first mate presented a breakfast of omelets, toast and sliced fresh fruit, all served on fine china with a silver pot of coffee. "Please signal if you need anything further, sir."

"This is nice," Erin said as she speared a wedge of cantaloupe from her plate.

"After everything we talked about last night, I thought it was a good idea for us to get some privacy. None of that was anybody's business but ours." With emotions flying, he'd worried that one of the gossip hounds would perceive the tension between them and start some kind of rumor. They both had enough eyes on them already. Especially as Erin had left the party with a sudden need to be alone. And not to mention the state of near swoon he'd been in dancing with her. Confirming that she still smelled like cream and the two of them melding into the single unit they used to be.

But now in the safety of the boat's cabin, Kento wanted to get it all cleared up and out in the open. At last. "So, last night, discussing your parents'…offer to me…"

"I know my parents are ruthless," she jumped in. "I've seen how they conduct business dealings. But I can't believe they'd sink so low as to offer you money to get you out of the picture."

"All this time, I thought you knew. They told me the three of you had talked it over and that you'd concurred it was for the best." Worse than Ingram and Bunny's cut-and-dried bribe, a disgusting bargain to affect two young hearts, was that they'd lied and told him Erin was in agreement. "How naive I was to take them at their word." As a matter of fact, it was only yesterday, upon finally seeing Erin again, that he'd flashed on the possibility that there was more than one version of what had transpired. His hunch had been right.

"If I was in cahoots with them, why wouldn't I have just broken up with you? Do you really think I would have agreed to a plan to buy you off?"

"I believed what they told me. I was a twenty-one-year-old kid," Kento said, all of it still sinking in. "They said you didn't love me."

Anguish changed her face. "How could you have taken that as truth?" Her voice cracked. "Hadn't you noticed? What we had was real for me. I never would have betrayed you. Give me a little more credit than that." Kento had no idea what lengths Erin would have gone to at her parents' behest. All he knew was that Ingram and Bunny had tight control over their daughter. And he hadn't even told her all that was said that day with her parents.

"Let's get some air." Erin got up and mounted the four steps to the boat's deck. Kento followed her as she made her way to the starboard side, wrapping her two hands around the railing and peering out into the distance. Kento took a stand right next to her. He'd been scorned and devastated, yet his gut was twisting that he had upset her. All this time, she'd thought he'd left her for reasons of his own. Because he didn't love her. In fact, the Barclays had bent things around so much he never knew that Erin was unaware of their horrible plot to get rid of him.

The boat moved in between two smaller islands on the Sound, dense with trees. Erin started to speak and then stopped herself. He didn't let it slide. "What were you going to say?"

She took in a slow inhale and let out an even slower exhale. Whatever she wanted to share wasn't coming easy. "All of the time we were together, my parents tried to brainwash me into distrusting you. They told me that people like you were looking for connections. For the opportunities that aligning with a family like mine might bring. I told them you'd never do anything like that, but they tried to get me to doubt your sincerity in even being with me."

As he took in her words, blood came to a boil through his veins. "How dare they tell you those kind of lies!" In another repeat from seven years ago, Kento was stunned at the lengths the Barclays would go to in order to maintain their private bubble. He'd never met people like that, who thought nothing of lying to and manipulating their own daughter. Kento slapped his hand against the railing, compelled to bang his anger out somewhere. Smacked it a second time.

"When you left for Tokyo, they assured me how right they were, that you only cared about me because I was a Barclay. And that once you figured out they weren't going to usher you into their life of standing and privilege, you left. Further proof that you'd never loved me in the first place."

Erin searched him, as confused as he was by all that had been said. Contemplating, trying to piece it together. Until she gasped. What had been teary eyes began to weep in earnest. Her cries carried off the boat deck, and the wails merged with the crashing of waves in the Sound.

"What is it?" he finally asked. "Why are you crying so hard?"

"I just *got it*," she sobbed. "You took the bribe. That's how you had the money to start your software company. No wonder you never reached out to me again after you got to Japan. NIRE was founded on my family's money."

Everything Erin had held on to for the past seven years turned to dust and scattered off the boat deck and into the waters of Puget Sound. This was Kento Yamamoto, a man so forthcoming and fair that he wouldn't even accept the meal assistance some of his university scholarships included, letting the aid committees know that his parents could provide food for him. How could that same person pocket a payoff from her parents to get out of their lives, all the while knowing it would break her heart in the process?

Which was the real man and which was the facade? Anything was possible. Maybe she'd glorified him too much and never saw who he really was. Could her parents have been right? After all, he didn't come to her, didn't meet her at that bakery to demand an explanation.

"Erin!"

She didn't turn her head, instead focusing her eyes on the waves.

"For heaven's sake, Erin!" he exclaimed until he shocked her out of her trance. "I didn't accept their attempted payout! Is that how little you think of me?"

"Oh, my gosh." Erin put her hand over her mouth to muffle her tears.

"Do you really think I'd have taken it?"

"Look at it from my point of view. Some-one who flees without a goodbye has surely done something wrong." Even though she tried to sync her eyes to his, now it was he who wouldn't look *her* in the face. He could be lying, but something deep in her soul as-sured her he wasn't. And he was certainly more likely to be honest than her parents were. "But no. You wouldn't have been part of a dirty deal like that. The possibility just popped into my mind. I shouldn't have voiced it."

"I built NIRE on nothing! My uncle Riku gave me an entry-level job after graduation. I started designing software at night and on the weekends, using every moment of my spare time to learn and develop. I'll tell you any-thing you want to know about my company, but I'll ask you not to make any assumptions."

Erin noticed the boat turning to begin its return to the harbor. They had to get back to their duties at Christy and Lucas's wedding. There was the ceremony rehearsal and then a rehearsal dinner. They had to get ready.

What a mess they'd unearthed in less than twenty-four hours. Thanks to her parents, she'd spent seven years thinking it was so easy for Kento to leave. In turn, he'd spent that time believing she hadn't loved him. It was a tragedy of misunderstanding. More tears began to form, ready to spill from her eyes. After the disaster with Harris, she was starting to genuinely realize that her parents' prescription for her life wasn't working out. She hadn't married, hadn't bred. They had failed at creating the next-gen socialite they wanted her to be. Hearing about their foul behavior years earlier was the icing on the cake.

And now she'd greatly offended Kento with her guess that he'd taken her parents' dirty money. They needed a way to put this all behind them and get on with the day. She eked out, "Forgive me for even acknowledging the possibility."

He was silent, and they both watched as the boat approached the dock.

"I think you might have to earn that forgiveness," he answered finally. Why did the way he'd said that sound more flirty than angry?

"How would I do that?" she flicked back, grateful he was lightening the mood.

With one of his long fingers, he tapped his cheek, indicating that he wanted Erin to kiss it right there. The gesture was both silly and thrilling, making Erin's spirit brighten, not to mention causing her stomach to tingle. Holding fast to his demand, he leaned down a bit, bringing his cheek closer to her. She lifted up on tiptoes and placed a prolonged but gentle kiss onto his cheek. His satisfied grin would have irked her if it wasn't so adorable.

Back at the lodge after their breakfast cruise, Kento and Erin parted to get ready for the rehearsal. Trying to pull all the pieces of the morning together, she showered and put on her outfit for the day. A silky, fitted silver T-shirt went nicely with the full skirt, also silver, that came together with a black belt and black ballet flats. As she was slipping on some bangle bracelets, Christy called and asked her to come to the dressing room in the main lodge, because she was having second thoughts about her own ensemble.

Erin helped her sort through some options, all in the vivid colors the bride gravitated toward. She settled on the blinding pink shantung dress originally bought for the occasion. Christy had just been having jitters.

The bridal party had been instructed to

meet outside at the wedding canopy for the rehearsal. The weather was dreary but not raining as staff members arranged rows of cushioned white chairs for the ceremony. Erin and Christy arrived last, and Lucas called out, "Oh, wow," at the sight of his intended in her bright pink dress. That it was the color of stomach medication didn't stop him from bending his head to one side as he gazed adoringly at his bride. It was cute how smitten he was. Erin sincerely hoped their affection would last a lifetime.

Christy donned the practice veil she'd been handed, and Billy, the photographer, snapped some candid shots. Kento stood beside Lucas. The best man wore a fine charcoal suit with a white shirt and no tie, his hair in its sexy tangle. He looked so tall and stylish, Erin had a moment's jealousy that it wasn't her wedding to him that everyone had gathered for. A wish that the past hadn't played out as it had. That, for once, her relationship was going right and the man she loved stood ready to declare his intention of eternal partnership, of staying rather than going.

True love was never going to happen for her—she wasn't even open to it. Most especially not with Kento and all of the bad blood that had been spilled. He was the very person who had destroyed her hope of devotion. Even though she hadn't known about her parents' horrible behavior, she'd learned that he was capable of leaving her in a blink. If he could just disappear once, she could never trust him not to do it again. As their prickly boat ride this morning proved, there was still so much hurt and misunderstanding between them.

Although, for the first time she could ever recall, Erin pictured herself as a happy bride, mired in flower selections and reception menus, excited to begin matrimony with her groom. Seeing Kento again reminded her of all of the whimsical little daydreams she used to have about him. Imagining them as an already-married couple. Participating in all of the tiny moments that added up to a lifetime together. The stylish but unfussy house they'd live in. Trips they'd take. She'd gone as far as envisioning beautiful children who were not only bequeathed with their father's good looks but with his brains and hardworking determination. No, she cautioned herself again. Those hallucinations were part of her history, and she needed to leave them there. What-ifs had no place between the two of them anymore. She was glad they'd cleared up some of her questions about the past, but there really didn't need to be anything more than that.

"Mother of the bride—" Suni, the wedding planner, began organizing the decided-upon processional "—you'll be the first to walk down the aisle and then take your seat. Mother and father of the groom will already be seated in the front row. Next are the bridesmaids and groomsmen in pairs down the aisle, and then the maid of honor and best man."

Who would all part at the altar. Next was the flower girl. And last would be Uncle Vernon and Christy walking to the head of the aisle, where Lucas waited to meet his bride. As was traditional, Erin would hold Christy's bouquet as needed during the ceremony. Kento would be in charge of the rings, as Christy had opted not to have a bearer. "Everyone will run through the ceremony twice with me to make sure the placements are correct."

When it was their turn, Kento presented

the crook of his arm for Erin to take as they began their promenade according to instructions. While they did, his revelations on the boat this morning came flooding back, angering her to the point of distraction. But the best man and maid of honor strolled in the slow step of a formal processional—one foot forward, the other one meeting it. *Step, together, step, together.*

They'd explained so much to each other, yet she was still tormented. All of this happily-ever-after wedding business was just making her more and more incensed about her parents' inconceivable bribe. About her falling for their cover-up. At Kento for not having enough confidence in her to know that there was a limit to her condoning of her parents' behavior. That she wasn't a monster like they were. She would never have participated in a plot so evil as to let them buy off Kento. But was that true? While they'd never done anything quite so reprehensible, she'd had no record of standing up to them.

In reality, she desperately wanted to break away from them, to go her own way. Kento was the one who had planted that seed in her long ago, encouraged her to think for herself.

To question whether the attitudes held by her insulated parents, who'd never known toil and struggle, were accurate, fair, real. It was only now, being reunited with him, that brought those feelings back to the surface. Because when Kento left, it was as if he took the key to her cage with him, as if the gumption and fight he gave her flew out the door along with him. Not even realizing what she was doing, without Kento she'd walked right back into the prison of her parents' life.

"You still haven't explained why you didn't come to me after my parents tried to pay you to go," she blurted into his ear as they walked down the aisle, not censoring herself. "You believed them, believed that I would have gone along with their sickening scheme to get rid of you. Without even asking me. That's what you thought of me?"

"A bit slower, please," Suni called out. Kento adjusted his pace, and Erin followed suit.

"Is this really the time and place?"

"I don't care anymore, Kento." At this point, she didn't.

"If you hadn't known about what I've already told you, then you surely don't know the rest of it," he whispered.

"What are you talking about?" *Step. Together. Step. Together. Smile.*

"Your parents also informed me that I was lucky they were even offering me money. That if I didn't take their generous graduation present and immediately go away and never contact you again, they had some other actions they were prepared to take."

Erin's head whipped to look at him while he managed to keep them at the processional pace. "They threatened you?"

"Your father said they had been looking at a property on 4934 Spruce Street in Tacoma."

"Why would he say that?"

"You've been there. The address is the building where my parents' grocery store occupied the ground floor. The shop they'd owned and operated for thirty years. Your father told me he was thinking of buying the building for a teardown. To build condos." *Step. Together. Step. Together.* "After all that time there, my parents wouldn't have been able to start over somewhere else."

Erin felt light-headed, nauseous.

After a few breaths to collect her wits, she

said, "I wish you'd never met me in that philosophy class." *Step. Together. Step. Together.*

"I don't feel that way. The year we had together was…"

"I mean," she interjected, "if we had never met, my parents couldn't have treated you so horribly."

She was shocked, mortified. Embarrassed to even be the offspring of thugs who would go to such lengths. They thought it was all for her own good, for the good of the family. With their own laws to answer to. But it sickened her nonetheless, that they would have terrified this upstanding young man who'd already had doors slammed in his face, who'd been said no to countless times. How people so fortunate could be so heartless was baffling.

He tilted his head in resignation. "I suppose I should thank you for that sentiment?"

"Can you understand how much you destroyed me by leaving rather than coming to me with all of this?" *Step. Together.*

"I was just a kid!" His voice rose and then he corrected it. "I was being crushed myself. Regardless of how you felt about me, I assumed it wasn't enough to make you defy them."

Erin used her pinkie finger to dab at the corners of her eyes. *Smile.*

"Are you all right?" Billy inquired.

"Everything is just so beautiful," Erin quickly fibbed. "I always cry at weddings."

Billy snaked left, right and sideways.

Once the maid of honor and best man reached the altar, they parted. Erin joined the bridesmaids on Christy's side of the aisle. It was agonizing to leave Kento's side, Amber and the girls looking on. Kento slapping a fake smile across his face reminded Erin to do the same. He took his place beside the groomsmen, with Lucas standing proud as he watched his bride in her pink dress walk toward him on her father's arm.

Of all the merciless and cutthroat things Erin knew her parents did in their business dealings, what they had done to Kento took the prize. The Barclays did as the Barclays saw fit. They were afraid of no one; their cold hearts kowtowed to no one.

Bunny and Ingram had decided their daughter's future, and Kento had no place in it. That was that. A mutually beneficial marriage was key. A merging of dynasties, another business agreement. They hadn't even given her a real place in the company. She'd thought she had a knack for finding interesting historic properties for sale and wished she could direct her energies toward that, but they had never allowed her in. It had already been formally documented that while she would eventually inherit Barclay Properties, she would not be put in charge of its operations. Gender roles still prevailed, even in her mother's mind. Male cousins were being groomed for the key positions when the time came.

After Christy and Lucas took their places, everyone participated in a practice of the ceremony. Erin pretended to help the bride with the imaginary train of her gown. She took Christy's bouquet to hold for her, today made of plastic flowers provided by the wedding planner. Suni stood in for the officiant and ad-libbed some vows. Kento mimed handing Lucas the wedding rings.

Once the rehearsal had been completed twice, the wedding party did their second recessional back down the aisle. Kento and Erin joined arms again. During the short intervals, she'd missed resting her hand around his rock-solid bicep.

Billy was at the end of the aisle, shooting

everyone on their return walk. "Let's have a cheek-to-cheek photo of the maid of honor and the best man."

MacKenzie, Amber and Divya craned to get a good view.

"I can't stop thinking about what you must have gone through, with me disappearing into thin air and you not knowing why," he said, resuming the conversation Erin thought was over. She brought her cheek against his, which was warm and clean shaven. "You asked me to forgive you for thinking that I might have accepted your parents' money. Now it's my turn to ask you for forgiveness. For not coming to you back then, for choosing to silently run away."

Erin was dumbstruck by the simplicity and humility in his request. Given all of the circumstances, she thought she could forgive. Although she'd never forget.

After the rehearsal, the wedding party joined other guests, who mulled about on the lawn and on the large patio with its firepits. Some people made s'mores with the fixings provided, toasting the marshmallows over the open fires with long sticks. Others enjoyed green appletini cocktails from the bartender's station. Kento got called into conversation by some flashy women. Erin saw Bunny coming toward her. Her mother was just plain fortunate that there were a lot of people around, or else she might have started a shouting match. As it was, she shot her mother a vicious glower.

"Erin, there's someone I want you to meet." Bunny charged in, obviously not reading her daughter's mood. Or, more accurately, not caring.

"I had a little chat with Kento this morning," Erin spat in staccato. "It seems there were some events from the past I had no knowledge of."

"Mmm, yes, well, your father and I made some choices at the time that we thought were in everyone's best interest."

"Yeah, I heard. You threatened and intimidated a twenty-one-year-old whose only crime was loving me. Great decision."

"Do you see that gentleman over there?" Bunny ignored Erin's words and pointed one spindly finger in an indiscreetly discreet way to a small man in a black suit standing with a group of suited men. Erin estimated him to be fifteen or so years older than her. His upper lip curled under as he rapidly shook his head in agreement at what someone was saying, making him look like an eager mouse. "That's who I was telling you about. Humphrey Colder. Big oil money. His family worked with the Alaskan pipeline and all that implies. They own half of Fairbanks."

"Mother, do you hear me? I am livid, not to mention heartbroken, about what you did to Kento after graduation, and that you lied to me about it."

"And don't you understand me, dear? Humphrey Colder is the type of match we need to make. You and Kento had your college fling, fine. But we certainly weren't going to let you continue to associate with a young man unsuitable as a marriage prospect. It just wasn't prudent."

"Prudent! Good heavens, can you hear yourself? Are you heartless?"

"Barclays look forward, not back. Go introduce yourself to Humphrey." Bunny put her brittle hand between Erin's shoulder blades to give her a push in the man's direction. Out of the corner of her eye, she saw Kento watching the entire exchange, too far away to hear them but seething nonetheless.

Surrounding him were several women trying to get his attention, but his eyes were on her.

"Didn't she know his reputation? He never stays with any woman for too long."

"I heard they lasted six months. That must have been a record for him."

Kento overheard two of the wedding guests talking about Erin as she walked by. This crowd certainly loved gossip. He'd been over-hearing comments left and right about poor Bunny, whose daughter hadn't been able to find a husband. And when he watched Bunny steer Erin toward a man who was clearly too old and stodgy for her, Kento snarled in disgust.

Not that he was faring much better. As soon as the rehearsal was over and the bridal party joined other guests, the glamazons sur-rounded him in a swarm. The discussion seemed to center on how many carats Christy's diamond ring had and did he know where Lucas had bought it? Once he saw Erin break from the man her mother insisted she meet, Kento pulled away and toward her, along the way grabbing a couple of the pretty green ap-pletinis in stemmed glasses.

"Fed to the lions?" he asked as he handed her the drink.

"My mother simply could not wait another moment to introduce me to a bore who smells like garlic."

"Helpful to ward off vampires?"

"Very funny." She took a sip of the sweet and tart drink. "This is good."

"In everything we've said to each other, I don't know if I've stated clearly enough how sorry I am that I didn't confront you seven years ago about what your parents did. It's something that has haunted me for years, even without all of the new information. If I had, then neither of us would have spent all of this time with hurts and resentments based on falsehoods."

"That's for sure."

He was startled by her bluntness but almost proud of her for it. "How can I make it up to you?"

"You can't. It's too late." She was right, yet her words cut like a knife. Another thought occurred to him. How much had his leaving influenced the way she related to men in general? Was she expecting to be disappointed by any man she might date, therefore creating a self-fulfilling prophecy? Had his own actions not only held him back from developing any meaningful relationships but done the same to her? Guilt racked through him. Bad enough that Erin had merciless parents who controlled her, but Kento had come along and made everything worse with his desertion. What could he do for her that would be a gesture of repentance, some way he could be of service to her?

Christy swooped in and said into Erin's ear loud enough for Kento to hear, "Do you see that man making the s'more over there?" She gestured to a beefy bald guy who was frustrated when he set his marshmallow on fire so badly it turned to black ash. "He's another excellent prospect. Scooter Markinson. Of the Markinson department stores! Go talk to him."

Erin looked at Christy with wide eyes to try to indicate she didn't want this conversation to be happening in front of Kento, which he could understand. It would be humiliating to have people trying to matchmake right in front of someone important from your past. Didn't these people have any tact? That was something he could say about

Japan—people were for the most part polite in front of each other regardless of what they might be thinking inside. In any case, the marshmallow torcher was nowhere near good enough for Erin—he could tell that from first glance.

An idea popped into his head. It might not have been a smart one, in fact, it probably wasn't, but it was a notion nonetheless.

"I can't undo the past, but I just thought of a way I could help you out now," he said after Christy moved on.

"With what?" She took a sip of her drink and then licked her lips. Instant proof that what he was thinking wasn't a good plan, because it would involve not wanting to kiss the drops of appletini right off her. And he wasn't sure he was capable of that if she insisted on having such a sexy mouth all the time.

"Remember you had said you wished you had a date to the wedding so that the marriage brokers and gossip mongers would see that Harris didn't trample you? That you're still a catch." *To say the least.*

"Yeah."

"What about me? What if you and I pretended to be back together? That would get everyone off your back, wouldn't it?"

"You and I?" Her eyebrows furrowed. "That would be too weird, wouldn't it?"

"It would just be pretend, right? Only when we were around people. We could pull it off."

"I don't know."

"Almost everyone here knows we have a past together. And they must assume we've remained friendly, or else how could we stand as maid of honor and best man? And…"

"Slow down a minute, will you?" She was trying to grasp the concept even as Kento reeled at his own crazy suggestion. The two of them posing as a couple was a terrible prospect. Unless it wasn't. What if it even benefited him in his initial quest for this weekend? To get over her, once and for all. Maybe the proximity of pretending to be a couple would be the final capstone on feelings that had lingered for too long. Playacting for a short time could help him find the closure he was seeking.

"It would get the leeches off me for the weekend as well, right?"

"I suppose so," she pondered. "What,

we'd just tell people that we'd gotten back together?"

"Yeah. Things like that happen to people all the time at weddings. The romance brings it out in them."

He sounded like he was reading from a promotional brochure.

"I see."

"Then what? After the weekend is over?"

"We'll leave telling everyone that we'll be traveling back and forth to see each other as much as possible."

"I'm not sure pretending like that would be a good plan."

"What about your parents? They would be vehemently against you and I getting back together. The mere idea of that would infuriate them."

A cat that swallowed the canary's smile slowly widened across Erin's face. "Now, that it would."

CHAPTER FIVE

JUST AS KENTO'S proposition was starting to
sink into Erin's brain, the photographer sidled
up to them. "I need to test some light at the
wedding altar. Christy and Lucas are visiting
with some family that has just arrived. Can I
get you to come with me and stand in for the
bride and groom?" Naturally, they obliged.
As they walked across the lawn to the site,
she contemplated the proposal.

"Harris Denby. The crazy one who drinks
champagne from the bottle." She watched a
less than subtle couple point at her with no
shame whatsoever.

Although Erin appreciated Kento's offer,
especially as he meant it as a peace offering,
she was very skeptical. While it might make
the weekend outwardly easier, it was already
a lot to see him again, let alone act as if they
were back together.

A number of guests looked on while Billy positioned them as bride and groom for the ceremony. Grabbing the practice veil that Christy had rehearsed with earlier, he placed it on Erin's head with the top layer cloaking her face. He also handed her the plastic bouquet, which she held in both hands like a proper bride. "Great. Gaze lovingly at each other and I can check for shadows."

Gaze lovingly was not a hard command to fulfill. What took concentration was how hard she had to work at not picturing the moment differently. Billy was looking for shadows. She knew exactly where they were. It was as if all the secrets and lies that had just come forward had served to bring her and Kento closer to each other than they'd ever been, even more than seven years ago. With the maturity of adults, they could analyze the damage that had been done to both themselves and each other. The disappointment and melancholy were all the more profound when shared by two people who were too shattered to ever stand at an altar in wedding clothes.

"Kento, can you lift Erin's veil as if you were the groom?"

But what if this was real? That she'd get to have Kento, to have and to hold, for the rest of her life? Something that was never going to happen. He dutifully raised the tulle and smoothed it behind her head with a tenderness that was almost tragic.

What about his offer, though? If she took him up on it, presumably she wouldn't have to be galloped around like a thoroughbred for the rest of her time on the island. Nor be pitied by the snobs who laughed at her gullibility in partnering with Harris. It would help Kento keep the gold miners away, too. And most importantly, it would incense her mother, and a little revenge would taste sweet in Erin's mouth right about now. All short-lived, but what did she have to lose?

Except for one thing. How on earth would she act as if she was with Kento without conjuring up the longing for something decidedly unphony? Embarking on this could be a cruel make-believe. Looking into his luminous, captivating eyes, she knew she'd have to take care not to be destroyed by him for the second time when this was over and he went back to Japan alone.

Billy took her bouquet and adjusted the two

of them a little closer. "Blah, blah. Blah, blah, you may now kiss the bride."

Erin noticed Bunny standing farther back on the lawn with her friends but turning her head toward the altar. The bridesmaids and groomsmen watched in a gaggle, all holding their appletinis. The mousy garlic man, the bald s'mores maker and just about every guest clustered around turned their attention to the scene.

Kiss the bride.

Kento took her face in his hands. She reached her arms around his neck. Was she about to playact as Billy had asked them to? Or were they embarking on the more complex charade that Kento had suggested? If they made this kiss convincing, it could kick off the ruse he was suggesting. With so many people's eyes on them, it could serve as the announcement that the maid of honor and best man were once again a real-life couple.

If so, it should be a kiss that looked passionate, yet the two of them would know it was only for show. She'd watched enough movie smooching that she could imitate how to press her whole mouth against his and rotate her head a little as if he was rubbing the kiss in. That way it would look like he was giving her a deeply romantic kiss. He'd understand what she was doing and follow along. As a matter of fact, they should remember how they did it, because it was a tool they'd be utilizing throughout the wedding weekend. Okay. This could work, she told herself.

Unfortunately, though, that's not how it went.

In fact, he urged his mouth against hers with a force that made her instantly lose concentration on the task at hand. His lips found hers, certain where to go, as if no time had passed. A two-piece puzzle that easily fit together into a groove. His mouth was even more persuasive than she had remembered, and her resolve to control the kiss was obliterated. His lips insisted hers open, and he circled his tongue around hers. Her knees buckled. She was in big trouble.

There was no level of pretend going on, no matter which game they were playing. Her body jutted into his, unable to contain her physical reaction. And in pressing herself against him she could feel his firm physique beneath his clothes, reminding her, all but taunting her mind to replay the days and nights of intense, inexhaustible heat that they had once shared.

She hadn't had a chance to truly consider how much she would still respond to him. It was too late now, though, as the kiss, in front of everybody to boot, effectively answered the question as to whether or not they were going to enact the charade. In fact, the kiss swirled on far too long, their bodies becoming one being. The world all but disappeared until finally the sound of voices slowly reached her ears.

"Kento?"

"Kento?"

"Kento!"

"So the two of you are a real-life couple," a man said to Kento with a wink to Erin as he entered the rehearsal dinner. The best man and maid of honor greeted guests as they filed in for the evening, which was to include a show.

Kento had barely recovered from what transpired on the lawn a few hours ago. Since then, he and Erin had been busy with helping Lucas and Christy rework the table arrangements, as one couple unexpectedly brought their children, who hadn't been included in the head count. Also, Christy wasn't happy with the hors d'oeuvres samples, so they met with the chef to modify them to her satisfaction.

All that hadn't left him with much time to review his moves. Erin had never even answered him about whether she wanted to playact that they were a couple. He'd decided for them. At the altar, standing in for the bride and groom as they were pronounced husband and wife, he'd intended to give her a kiss that *did* let everyone know they were back together, but one that would assure the two of them it was only masquerade.

Instead, reuniting with her lips was more intoxicating than he could handle. Blood and arousal had coursed through him in equal measure. The challenge to pulling off the fake-boyfriend act would rest on his ability to be immune to her charms. He was going to need to protect himself at every step. Because Erin was dynamite and could blow right through his plan to keep this phony. Worse still, he could easily envision her doing so. On top of it, he couldn't get the honeyed taste of her soft mouth off his tongue.

"I hope we'll hear wedding bells ringing in your future, too, someday," an elderly lady said to them.

"Do you know who she is?" Erin asked after the woman passed by.

"Not a clue."

"There are always a lot of the parents' friends in attendance," she whispered out of the side of her mouth. "Weddings are really for the moms."

"Don't tell that to my mine," Kento shot back as he greeted another stranger. "It's driving her nuts that I don't have a woman in my life. She's itching for grandchildren."

"Nice to see you. Take a seat anywhere," Erin continued her hellos.

"There's not a bad seat in the house," Kento followed along.

He'd never thought of himself as part of a married couple. After Erin and then, to a lesser extent, Ayaka, he figured trusting someone was out of the question. So what would be the point in marrying if not to have wholehearted faith in the other person? All of these revelations since he'd arrived on the island were making his head throb to the point that he could actually imagine himself taking wedding vows. Maybe it was no wonder why he chose that exact moment at the altar to initiate their supposedly fake union. He really needed to keep his facts separate from fiction.

Being Erin's husband would make Bunny Barclay his mother-in-law. Which was never going to happen. There would be nothing that woman would hate more than seeing her daughter married to him. To *new tech money*, as if those were forbidden words. As if there was something dirty or wrongly gained about his fortune.

There was some measure of comfort in confirming that Erin hadn't known about her father's threat to him, to undermine and ruin the life Kento's parents had worked for so long to create. He'd always suspected that she didn't know that part of what had occurred. It turns out she knew none of it. But even if she had, it wouldn't have been enough to have turned her against them. The Barclays were ruthlessly clever in convincing her that Kento didn't love her. That was their best strategy. Telling her that he was only out to use her for what her family could do for him. Now it was far too late to put the broken pieces back together. Genuine sorrow washed over him.

"You still haven't told me," Erin inquired as more guests filed into the dinner theater, "in all these years, have you been dating?"

"I've met a few women who wanted to get close." He knew that sounded harsh, but it was the truth. "I've learned to spot insincerity."

"Hello. Welcome."

"Good evening."

Once most of the crowd had taken seats at the tables that surrounded the stage, Kento and Erin slipped in and stood against the wall near the back doors in case they were needed. They surveyed the room while waiters delivered blue mugs filled with steaming broth made from locally caught clams to each table as a toasty welcome. A server handed two to Erin. She gave one to Kento, and they both had a sip of the salty, savory liquid.

"I suppose I've done a fair amount of dating," Kento continued as the mug warmed his hands. "There was a woman I was with for eight months."

"Not someone you thought of staying with, though?"

"No, and after Ayaka, I made it my policy not to let anyone near."

"She betrayed you?"

"Ayaka is a corporate executive, busy and driven. I thought we were more or less leading the same lives and would be compatible." Indeed, when he was introduced to Ayaka Sato at a business party three years ago, he'd thought maybe he'd met someone he could share his existence with. Although the connection he'd had with Erin still lingered on him like a perfume that overtook him and transported him back to Seattle, he'd needed to step out, and Ayaka seemed to come along at the right time. In his heart, he knew that his solitary life had led him to loneliness. That casual encounters with women here and there were completely unsatisfying. That it would be ultimately unhealthy for him, and for his empire, if he continued in isolation.

So when Ayaka's quick mind and high energy appealed to him, he began dating her. At first only once every couple of weeks, because he'd never been dependent on anyone besides Erin, and he wasn't ready to risk being hurt again. But when the companionship proved pleasant, and Ayaka was more than willing, he increased their get-togethers to once a week. "We're dating, and then she announces to me at dinner, out of the blue, that she wants to become pregnant with my child within the next three months."

"Wow." Erin's voice rose. "Just like that?"

"Yes. She said this was an optimal time in her career for her to have children. That she and her family had considered my lack of pedigree but given that I had built NIRE into such a prominent company, I must have genes that would be desirable for coparenting."

"Desirable genes… That's intense."

"It always turns out that every woman I meet wants something from me, is thinking of how she can benefit from me. I don't mean to sound arrogant, but do I read as desperate? Where did Ayaka get the impression that because she'd come to a verdict about having children it was a done deal?"

A jagged breath reminded him how angry that situation had made him. The years of judgment he'd endured growing up had only led to more, in subtle adult ways that were even more insulting than school hallway taunts. "After eight months," he went on, "I'd thought that maybe she and I had come to understand each other, that we'd opened up enough to show each other our real selves." Like what he'd had with Erin.

"But you were mistaken?"

"Yes. We'd only gotten as far as discovering we liked the same ice-cream flavor and political candidates. That wasn't really getting to know someone. And in the meantime, she, along with her parents, had been busy selecting me as a breeder."

"Well, I know all about having decisions made for me," Erin mused.

"Yes, you do."

She was forcing him into thoughts he hadn't had in a while. Before and after his time with Ayaka, he'd made sure to let any women he'd spent time with know up front that nothing serious would grow between them. Still, he had no trouble finding dates. In his world, filled with young people in the big city, there was an endless stream of attractive women charging toward him. He could hardly dismiss them fast enough. Everyone was measuring and trading and leveraging assets at all times, even if they didn't consciously realize that's what they were doing.

It had never felt like that with Erin, except

when he'd left Seattle convinced that she was in on her parents' plans to get rid of him. Before that, and now during this weekend, she brought out the parts of him that rarely saw the light of day. With her, he felt he could be natural and instinctive, almost innocent. Like the wholly inappropriate way he'd kissed her for the photographer. He could have easily given her the fake smooch he'd meant to. The savage, ravenous beast inside him had had other ideas. He knew he'd surprised her with the insistence of his lips. And all he could think about was wanting more. Craving it. Needing it.

However, practice would make perfect. How many times did he have to go over and over one of his new software programs until it ran like clockwork? This was the same. Soon enough, he'd be immune to Erin's kisses and they'd be able to play their roles to perfection. Once he got used to her again, she'd no longer have such an effect on him. It would be no problem to act like lovers for the weekend and then be out of each other's lives forever. No problem. At all.

Perhaps it was maturity that advised him, something innate that told him that he had magic with her, the kind that only comes around once in a lifetime. So he needed to watch out. Even standing next to her against the wall in the middle of this wedding fanfare, she made him feel connected. Almost daring to think that all the destruction of their past wouldn't matter an iota if he had her.

Lucas and Christy entered the theater, followed by the groomsmen and bridesmaids. Kento and Erin would sit with them once their greeter duties were done. He'd made sure to confirm to Demarcus that he and Erin had rekindled their romance, knowing word would continue to spread to the all of the guests.

"Ladies and gentleman…" A voice broke in over the loudspeaker. "Welcome to Locklear Lodge's *Song of the Golden Eagle*, a celebration of the Native American peoples who first populated the Pacific Northwest. In a few minutes, you will be enjoying our presentation of welcome dances. That will be followed by our buffet dinner, with a menu inspired by foods that might have been eaten by the first inhabitants of the island. Prepare to feast on fresh salmon cooked on cedar planks over an open fire, grilled squash, our corn and lima bean succotash, and molasses bread. After that, our resident storyteller will share tales of his ancestors, to be followed by our performers, who will dance, drum and chant wearing native dress and masks."

They both watched as Bunny sat down at a table with her friends.

"Will you talk to your mother about what you've unearthed?"

Erin's sarcastic resignation of them was a front, but to his knowledge she'd never taken any real steps toward freedom. Which pained him greatly. Even if he wasn't going to spend the rest of his life with her, he'd wish her one of independence. An existence without it was slavery.

"I already did, at the marshmallow roast." She shrugged. "It was in my best interest, and to protect our holdings and all that. Which I need to respect. Nothing will ever change with them," she added with a chin-up gesture that was somehow excruciating.

"As expected."

"I don't really care what she thinks anymore."

Kento knew that wasn't accurate, but he liked the sound of it.

When her mother glanced over to them,

Erin went up on her tiptoes and brought her lips to his, continuing what they had started a few hours earlier on the lawn. Kento squinted out of the corner of his eye to watch as Bunny's expression turned enraged.

But then he stopped noticing Bunny and got lost in the fervor of Erin's kiss, which sent hot lava bubbling up through his body.

The guests enjoyed their dinner. For dessert they were served Native American fry bread, discs of dough that had been browned in oil and topped with jams and honey. At each place setting was a party favor to take home. It was a dream catcher, a small wooden hoop made into a net with fibrous crisscrossing threads and adorned with beads and feathers. The storyteller explained that dream catchers resemble a web, and that spiders are considered symbols of protection and comfort in some cultures. They are sometimes hung over a baby's crib while they sleep, as they were believed to keep bad dreams away and let good ones in.

During the show, Erin found herself stroking the dream catcher with her thumb. All of what had gone on with Kento and her parents was like a nightmare that kept repeating in her head. Maybe the party favor could help put the past to rest.

After the performance guests began to retreat to their lodgings, anticipating the wedding day ahead. Kento and Erin spent some time with the bride and groom, making sure everything was in order and that they weren't suffering from anything other than typical wedding butterflies. Both seemed happy, excited, nervous and tired all at once, and they were looking forward to a good night's sleep. Erin advised, "Hang the dream catcher on your bedpost tonight." She figured it couldn't hurt.

"I'll walk you to your room," Kento said as the two of them left. A floor of suites in the main lodge was being used by the bridal party, although she knew that he had instead booked one of the luxury private cabins for himself.

"Should we take a little walk first?"

"Sure."

She wasn't ready to part company with him just yet. All of what had gone on today was tangled in her head. One fact she was having trouble grappling with was that in spite of hearing about all of the atrocious actions she'd never known about, her heart had begun to sing again.

As they strolled the footpath that surrounded the lodge's main buildings, the night was quiet and Erin had more to say. "I'd always considered you leaving after graduation an absolute rejection."

Kento mashed his lips together in distress at her words. "Of course, when you hadn't known that there were bribes and threats."

"That's more than a young man could have been expected to combat."

"Your parents, in their own twisted way, subscribe to family loyalty and realized I did as well. So they figured out how to leverage that to overtake me and send me packing."

"It made sense that you fled to Tokyo when you had the chance. In addition to being outright scared by the menacing threat to destroy your parents' life, you probably left, in part, to protect me."

"I can't say it didn't occur to me. I was afraid that if you defied your parents and persisted in being with me, you'd have to break from them completely. That's a big decision that might never, ever have been reversed."

"You mean, if I turned my back on them, all their wealth and property and standing, what if it hadn't worked out between you and me?" He had no way of knowing at the time that he'd become the success he did. Which didn't guarantee happiness, anyway. "What if I regretted it later? What if I was left with nothing? And what if that was in Japan, where I'd be completely alone?"

"And your parents were just merciless enough to let that happen."

By vanishing, Kento had been thinking ahead, covering every possibility in what he thought was best and safest for her.

Something that had come right back between them was how they cut to the quick of their feelings. "This reminds me of the old days. I was more honest with you than I've ever been with anyone before or since."

"I was my most real with you, too," he agreed. "Except when it mattered most."

"There's the ultimate irony."

In a way she would never act on, she wished for more from him. As if by his side, she could conquer the world. All these years later, she would be ready for his wisdom and strength to help her escape her jail, escape from living like a half woman, half child, prized only if she produced heirs. Facing how truly brutal her parents were, she didn't know how she was going to be able to return to their Seattle mansion after she'd packed up the remains of the Harris Denby disaster in Spokane. She'd have to ask her dream catcher tonight to bring her an entirely new life.

As they strolled, she was certainly in no hurry to get back to her room. Who in their right mind wouldn't want to spend as much time as possible with this warm-blooded, smart, sexy, soulful man? Kissing him was electrifying, and she couldn't resist doing it again in the theater. With her mother watching, no less. She was bothered, aroused, alive, in his presence. Her assumption that they could play at this for the weekend and that it would mean nothing afterward was fading away.

"Where on the grounds are the cabins?" she asked as they rounded a corner. She knew that Kento had booked the biggest one for the bride and groom, although for tradition's sake Christy would sleep there alone tonight with Lucas in a suite in the lodge.

"Come on, I'll show you." He gestured

down a walkway that led away from the main buildings.

They reached the dozen or so cabins, built far apart from each other for privacy on the expansive grounds.

"This is a lovely and secluded setting. What are the cabins like inside?"

"Country charm meets highbrow—what else would you expect? There's an outdoor shower."

Erin was most definitely not thinking about Kento naked under the outdoor tap when she asked, "Have you used it?"

"As a matter of fact, I have," he answered with a hint of a smile that made her curious. A moment's silence fell between them under the dark night sky. After what seemed like a contemplation, he finally asked, "Do you want to see my cabin?"

Trepidation prickled her body. They both knew that if she visited his cabin, there was every possibility that the shell of their masquerade would become even further cracked than it had been by the unfake kisses they'd already shared. In a couple of days, Kento would board his private jet and she would probably never see him again as long as she lived. Would taking their intimacy further be the crescendo of goodbye to the only man that had she ever cared about, or would it make the pain of their saga even more profound and unlivable?

"Yes," she answered in almost inaudible whisper. Yes, physical connection with Kento again would be worth the heartache it would surely cause. It was past an option for her. It had become inevitability.

He took her hand as they walked, which felt only too good. When they reached his cabin, he helped her up the porch steps and released her hand while he fished in his pocket for the key card to swipe open the front door. Once inside, he used one foot to help the other out of its shoe and then reversed it to take off the second. Erin remembered that he'd always observed the Japanese custom of removing shoes when inside his home. With a chew to her lip and her body a bundle of nerves, she took off her shoes as well and placed them next to his just inside the doorway. How they looked together! His big black dress shoes next to her much smaller black ballet flats.

She hoped he'd make small talk, although that wasn't his style. He was well aware that she wasn't in his cabin for a nightcap. Nor to see the paintings on the wall. She could still read him enough to know that he was leaving this up to her. He wasn't going to throw himself on her. But she also registered the lust in his eyes. Telling her he wouldn't refuse her tonight.

"Kento."

That's all she wanted to say. Wanted to hear the sound of his name out loud, hanging in the air. He bent down so that she could bring her lips to his. Caution rang in her, begging her to reconsider. This could be a mistake that she'd be burdened with forever. His life was five thousand miles away. What about the loneliness she'd feel when he left again, just to have shared their bodies one last time? Yet she couldn't stop herself. Being with him was the best thing she'd ever known. No one could blame her for craving a small taste of it again.

His hands traced down her spine as he finally pulled her tight, reassuring her that she was as desired as he was. He urged himself against her and she molded to him, their bodies together forming a perfect seal. His mouth moved from her lips to her jaw and then to her neck, where his teeth caught a bit of her

skin, causing her to moan. Prompting him
to continue as a quiet stream of pleasure vi-
brated low in her throat. His lips made their
way just under the neckline of her silky T-
shirt, and he flicked his tongue all the way
around the scoop.

Becoming urgent, his hands lifted the bot-
tom of her shirt out from its tuck into her
skirt so that he could have her bare skin. His
palms flattened against her back and then
circled around to her rib cage. Which wasn't
enough, and so he skimmed the shirt over her
head and off her, tossing it to a nearby chair.
And quickly removed her bra so that her entire upper body was without barrier. His wide
hands completely covered her breasts, making tingles dance all over her.

He looked her in the eyes, arousal hooding
his, to ask, "Do you want to see the outdoor
shower?" Her smile answered the question.

Leading her toward the door to the side
porch, he grabbed a stack of towels from the
bathroom along the way. Once outside, he
flicked on the standing heaters, which immediately began their task of metering the
chilly night.

Face-to-face again, Erin unbuttoned his

white dress shirt and slipped it off his shoulders. Her hands lingered on his bare, smooth chest, not the same as it had felt years ago. He was somehow both more muscular yet leaner than he used to be. Rediscovering him was thrilling. As they kissed again, she felt him work at the belt of her skirt, which he then carefully unzipped and helped her step out of. She slid off her underwear as he removed everything else he had on. With only a few lights to illuminate the area near the shower, his body glowed, alert and potent.

Turning on the tap, he eased her under the faucet so that the hot water flowed down her body. His wet hands felt her all over, as if they were committing her every curve and crevice to memory. Her body yielded to his every move, silently begging him not to stop even for a second. She'd never had a sexual experience with anyone that was even close to what she'd had with him at such a young age, intense and united and uninhibited. Both were each other's first lovers. How shocking it was that here they were revisiting that joining like a favorite travel destination they had to see again.

She wondered if she seemed different to

him after all this time, as he did to her. He slid his hand between her legs, fingers exploring. Her center clutched down on him, dying for this, dying for him. They thrummed together like musicians playing the same tune. Just when she thought she might not be able to take any more without exploding, he dropped down to his knees so that his mouth and tongue could cover her very womanhood. And there he gloried with the spray of the water raining down on them, the heavy drops rolling along his dripping hair to his taut body and glinting skin. As soon as he found the right groove, he stayed put until she threw her head back and her torso rollicked over and over again with blinding pleasure. After which she could barely stand.

Once the tremble passed through and she steadied, he wrapped her in two big, fluffy, white towels and lifted her into his arms. He carried her back into the cabin, into the bedroom, where he placed her down on his king-size bed with its many plush pillows. Admiring her like she was the most beautiful sight he'd ever seen, he reached in his travel bag for a condom, unrolled it onto himself and laid his body on top of hers.

CHAPTER SIX

IN THE MORNING, Kento opened the front door of his cabin to find the breakfast tray he'd called for. He carried it into the bedroom, where Erin was just stirring, looking so sleepy and pretty it tugged at his heartstrings. It was really almost too much to grasp that she had been in his bed again after all this time, which sent his mind back to all-night erotic encounters when they couldn't get enough of each other and he could scarcely grant her a minute's rest after lovemaking until they were at it again, hungry for more.

This was stuff that belonged in fairy tales. Things like long-lost loves didn't happen in real life. Although there she was, no longer merely the mythological siren who'd inhabited his visions. What had happened so far this weekend had truly brought him face-to-face with the reality of her. Not the milky recollections he'd traveled to Seattle to re-visit so that he could leave them behind. Be-cause making love with her didn't feel like something he was going to want to leave in the past.

He worried that the result would be the re-verse of what he intended, which was to for-get her.

He snatched the single pink rose from its vase that had graced the room service tray. Sitting at the edge of the bed, he brushed the velvety bloom across Erin's cheek as a wake-up call. She smiled but squirmed away. He chased after her with the flower, this time using it to stroke the shoulder that peeked out from the blankets. "Maid of honor, it's wedding day."

Her eyes clicked wide-open like a cartoon character's. "Oh, my gosh. Are we late?"

"We're due in the main lodge for the morn-ing get-together." The bridal party had been instructed to meet for some kind of shared ac-tivity to begin the big day on the right footing. Kento hoped it wasn't some kind of guided meditation where he was going to have to listen to his breath for half an hour or some-thing like that. After the night he'd just shared in carnal ecstasy with Erin—which a hunch told him he shouldn't have—the last thing he wanted to do was check into his thoughts. "Do you know what this is all about?"

"Nope."

"Up and going, missy." He pulled back the blanket both to shock her awake and also because he wanted to see her naked body again.

"You are sneaky," she shrieked.

"I am. Do you want to shower?" At that, they smirked, remembering the erotic encounter under the outdoor shower last night.

"I'll go back to my room, because I have to change into casual clothes. After the mystery activity, the girls have hair and makeup, and you have a final tux fitting."

They downed a quick breakfast, and Erin departed. As agreed, an hour later he knocked on her door to accompany her to the lodge's lounge, where they entered arm in arm as the couple everyone thought they were. It turned out the group was to participate in a nature drawing class, designed to *destress*, as explained by Suni, the wedding planner.

Kento didn't hate the plan. After Erin left to get changed and he showered, this time indoors and alone, a muddle of emotions had brought confusion to his usually organized brain. He'd just made shattering love with her after years of hurt feelings on both of their parts. They were both closed off to love because of each other. What a paradox that the only person he'd ever wanted to be committed to was the very one who'd killed his belief in the practice. Tomorrow he'd go back to Japan with no reason to return to Seattle. Erin and he were supposed to be posing as a couple, not becoming one! All together, he was in the middle of one hot mess. A drawing class, with a break from words, sounded like as good an idea as any.

As soon as they walked in, he and Erin sprang into action as maid of honor and best man, making sure that everyone received an apron to wear and was ushered to a place. Easels were set up for each person, along with sketch paper, pencils and erasers.

An art teacher, her apron pockets overflowing with extra supplies, circled around, introducing herself as Natasha. "Lucas and Christy, up here." Erin pointed to two easels front and center facing the glass wall.

While Erin was directing traffic, Kento took it upon himself to help her into her apron. He slung the strap over her head. She quickly glanced his way to acknowledge his doings and then continued, "Mother of the bride, let's have you over here." She gestured to her aunt Olivia.

Carefully lifting Erin's hair out from under the apron's strap, he appreciated probably far too much the way her shoulders rose at his slightest touch. Tugging on the waist strings, he enjoyed even more the feeling of circling them around her, giving a few extra pulls for emphasis.

Yes, he was ready to tie her up like a bundle, carry her back to his cabin and lay her down on his bed, just as he had last night with the towels after their outdoor shower. He'd like her all to himself, and for as long as he wanted. Obviously there'd be none of that on wedding day—not to mention the fact that, if he was smart, he'd keep himself in check for the rest of the weekend. Running an enormous corporation, Kento well knew that it was the long game that was important, that no moves should ever be made that only benefited the short run.

"Mother of the groom. You come and sit up front, too."

He was glad that only the bridal party was in attendance and he wouldn't have to see Bunny's unfriendly face this morning. Maybe drawing could distract him from the bona fide anger toward her and her absent husband that slowly burned like acid in his throat. Having learned that what he'd held to be gospel all of these years wasn't exactly as he'd remembered it, there was a lot of new information to manage.

How he wished they could turn back time and try again. Maybe things would have ended up the same, but maybe not. As it stood, what had happened had left an indelible mark on both of them. It had convinced him he'd never marry, would never be able to count on someone or be sure what their motives were. Attitudes born from what he'd grown up around. For Erin, he'd become the first in a series of abandonments that left her permanently fractured, a guilt he'd have to live with.

Once everyone was settled in, Kento brought Erin to a couple of side-by-side easels. "Welcome to this very special morning," Natasha began with a gesture to Christy and Lucas, who beamed. Kento could hardly imagine what the excitement of a wedding morning would feel like to a groom. It wasn't a thought he'd ever entertained. He'd attended weddings in Japan, those of employees and business acquaintances. Some were Western-style. Others were traditionally Japanese, with the bride wearing a special white wedding kimono and headdress and the groom in a dark kimono adorned with his family crest. The wedding custom of san-san-kudo struck him as quite romantic, the ritual exchanging of cups of sake in a binding ceremony, a symbol of their union. Yet he'd never pictured himself in either that kimono or tux.

"Don't feel like you have to sit at your easel the whole time," Natasha continued and pointed to a side table with refreshments. "There's coffee and mimosas. We're just here to relax, have fun and learn a little bit about sketching nature. And no worries about the results, absolutely no judgments allowed," she said with a kind smile.

"Today we'll focus on drawing one of the trees that we see out our beautiful glass wall," Natasha said, continuing with the lesson, an easel beside her facing the students. "So pick out a single tree or a cluster of them. We have many specimens to choose from. Zero in on something that strikes your fancy. There are no rights or wrongs."

Strikes your fancy. Erin struck his fancy.

"Let's lift up our pencils now and create the trunk of the tree with two vertical lines. You can decide on the thickness of the trunk and on its height," Natasha instructed and demonstrated.

"I'm drawing a tree, but it's not as big and tall as my future husband," Christy exclaimed, loud enough for people around her to hear. Lucas's size was his most distinguishing feature. Everyone cooed. Kento side-eyed Erin. It occurred to him how hard this wedding must be for her, having just been left by a guy who was surely the world's biggest idiot for not appreciating her. Kento picked up his pencil and began to sketch.

Natasha walked around, counseling anyone who signaled for help with their drawing. "Take a close look at the tree you've selected. Every tree is special, very different from the one next to it. Take note of how the branches extend from your tree trunk. Vary the sizes and the tapers of those branches. They are all individuals."

Several people looked up for assistance, and Natasha acknowledged each of them. Kento enjoyed the work, not obeying the teacher's instructions but instead letting his pencil take him wherever it wanted to. It was indeed relaxing to sketch. As his pencil danced, he kept glancing over to Erin, who was involved at her easel as well, his eyes only willing to go a minute or two without peering at her again.

"And when you're ready, you can begin adding the foliage to your branches," Natasha said. "Hold your pencil flat against the paper and shade some of your leaves dark and some of them light to imitate sun and shadow."

Drawing, drawing, Kento's pencil moved fast, easily knowing where to use shade and what to emphasize.

"Now let's blend the base of the tree into its surroundings. How does the tree take root in the ground? Is there dirt or grass surrounding it?"

When time was up, Natasha asked if anyone would like to show their drawing to the group. MacKenzie, Amber and Divya all three raised their arms high, shaking their hands to get noticed. Natasha held up Divya's first, and everyone clapped politely. Kento didn't think the drawing was in a realistic scale. But Natasha found something to praise in each drawing. As she returned to the front of the class, she stopped at Kento's easel and took in what he'd created.

"Here's someone who took the idea of individualism to heart." Before he could stop her, Natasha lifted Kento's drawing for the class to see. There were oohs and aahs in response.

His sketch was not of a tree, or even a branch or leaf.

No, his was a finely drawn rendering of Erin's magnificent face.

"I'm *so* nervous," Christy shrieked as the stylist rolled a curling iron on her hair. "What if I trip? What if Lucas flubs his vows?"

"It'll be fine. Everybody here is on your side." Erin was having her hair fussed at beside Christy at the lodge's salon, its walls made of brick with brushed-nickel appointments. Studded silver-framed mirrors hung were hung in front of each styling chair, which were light blue leather. Erin reached sideways to give a reassuring squeeze to the bride's hand.

Thinking about the words she'd just spewed, Erin knew she didn't have anyone on *her* side. Sure, her parents would try to shield her from, let's say, an untimely death. But support her in what she might want? Only if it was in line with their own wishes. And Kento? Here today and then, literally, gone tomorrow, regardless of the intensity they'd shared since arriving on the island. She tried not to dwell on that. The party line they circulated was that they'd fallen back in love and would be visiting each other as much as possible. The rest would be figured out later.

Amber, Divya and MacKenzie had already had their hair blown, set and poufed and were being ministered to by the makeup artist. "When did all of this happen with you and Kento?" Christy asked. "You never even told me you were in touch with him."

Yikes. Erin knew the scrutiny was going to get complicated. She wouldn't confide in her cousin about the fake-out. Christy was a Barclay through and through, about to wed her stockbroker with family hopes that she'd soon give birth to the next generation of opulence. Erin didn't trust her not to report to her mother or aunt with any inside information. Boiled down, Erin had never been especially close with her cousin, and she wasn't about to start now.

"Oh, we started talking when he found out I was going to be your maid of honor," she bluffed. "I guess the old feelings resurfaced."

"Erin, that was so cute how Kento drew that picture of you instead of the trees," MacKenzie said as the makeup artist tested different shades of lipstick on the back of her hand. "You are so lucky."

Erin smiled, more to herself than anyone. If they only knew.

"Are there any *good* single guys at this wedding?" Divya bubbled.

"Demarcus Hall is nice," Amber piped up. "What do we know about him?"

"Christy," MacKenzie asked, "does he work with Lucas?"

"No. They coach kids' basketball together."

"Aw."

"Aw."

"Aw."

"Is he unattached?"

"I think so. We told him he was welcome to bring a date to the weekend."

"But he didn't!"

"He didn't."

"Didn't!"

The modern world. Someone found someone else attractive and then tried to suss out as much as possible about the other without directly asking. It was a surprise that these bridesmaids hadn't already cybersearched groomsman Demarcus to the point that they knew his income, the value of his home and where he went to school. Still, it was all probably better than the archaic arranged-marriage routine Erin's parents adhered to. Obviously, they should have better researched Harris and not relied on his parents' sales pitch for their son.

Kento had mentioned yesterday that he figured this wedding weekend was especially hard on her only a few weeks after her breakup. It really wasn't, as far as the subject of weddings, since she certainly didn't love Harris and hadn't pictured marrying him. It was the humiliation of being broken up with that hurt. Which was why playacting that she was back together with Kento was proving to be a successful distraction. People were still nosy enough to talk about the two of them as a couple, but at least the focus was off Harris, everyone in seeming agreement that new-world Kento was at least better for Erin than the reckless playboy. This charade was a really good idea.

Or was it?

It might have been if they'd stuck to the pretend part instead of writing a symphony with their bodies during the most divine love-making Erin had ever known. Things had always been exciting between her and Kento in that department. But what they'd shared last night was a mature eroticism that was so poignant and complete, it made their young adult eagerness of the past an unfair contrast. The rush she felt in her solar plexus was escalating. What they'd been sharing this weekend together, through all of their walks and talks and the uncovering of horrors, had burrowed deep into Erin's soul. The sheer rawness of it was terrifying.

It was far easier to imagine a loveless coupling, formed to carry on family names and fortunes, where emotions weren't ventured and, therefore, couldn't be lost. With Kento it was the opposite—to be with him was to live powerfully, as if every day counted. She was almost exhausted by all the feeling she'd done since arriving at this wedding.

What was on Kento's mind at this very moment as he had his tux fitting with the guys? She wondered if he was thinking about her as much as she was about him.

"So, Erin," Divya broke into her musings, "do you think you'll move to Tokyo?"

Which prompted a barrage of inquiries as everyone was being primped and prettied and polished and perfumed. "Would you live at Kento's or find somewhere new together?"

"Does he live in one of those high-rise apartments with all the lights on the buildings?"

"Do you speak Japanese?"

"Does he work 24/7?"

"Does he want kids?"

Eek! Erin didn't know how to respond to all that probing. She locked eyes with her own reflection in the mirror facing her salon chair. She knew better than to be wishing those questions really were hers to answer, but she couldn't stop herself.

"Bridal party, please help yourself to an energy-boosting light lunch," wedding planner Suni sang out as she entered the salon along with a food server wheeling a cart. All of which happened at the perfect time to divert everyone from their interrogation. At least for now. "Green tea to sip. There's spinach salad with avocados, walnuts and dried goji berries. Grilled chicken breast. And we've got some dark chocolate to snack on. All chosen for their health benefits. After hair and makeup, you'll be dressing for the ceremony."

"My dress is a little loose in the chest. Can I get an alteration?" Amber asked Suni. The bridesmaids' gowns were short-sleeved V-neck style on top, leading to a bias-cut skirt. Erin's was embellished with pearl piping to differentiate her maid of honor status. She'd been relieved that with Christy's tendency to dress over the top, the gowns weren't too gaudy. Although the neon-violet fabric wouldn't have been Erin's choice.

"Yes, we'll have someone here to do a final check on everybody."

As the bridesmaids moved toward the food, Erin gave herself one more stare down in the mirror. She'd continue to try to elude those difficult questions the girls had asked since she'd likely never see Kento again after this weekend. And she'd have no real reason to go to Japan. The thought of that was so profoundly somber it turned her perfectly made-up face to ash.

"Here comes the groom!" Kento and the groomsmen sang to the tune of "Here Comes the Bride" as Lucas exited the changing room in his tuxedo. The men's dressing room was a large space with tan-colored carpeting and comfortable furniture upholstered in several shades of brown. A central area was surrounded by tall mirrors arranged in a semi-circle so that ensembles could be inspected from every angle. With three groomsmen, one best man, one groom and six mirrors, there was a lot of male energy in the space.

Lucas looked every bit the proper groom in his black tux with its violet cummerbund and tie, the color chosen by Christy to match her bridal party's dresses. The tailor checked Lucas's fitting and pinned a few alterations here and there. The rest of the men had been checked over in their tuxes that echoed the violet tie but sans the cummerbund. They were back in jeans and T-shirts for the time being. Their boutonnieres were laid out on a table, a pale purple rose surrounded by lilac

tied with a plaid bow, a nod to the rustic surroundings. Kento's had two roses to denote
him as the best man.

The groom's hair had been styled stiff from
the multitude of products no doubt employed,
but it would stay put for the many photos in
the outdoor elements. Kento had allowed the
hairdresser to add a bit of hold to his mane.
He didn't know Lucas's attendants prior to
this weekend, although they were a jovial
enough bunch. Demarcus Hall was a buddy
from basketball coaching, Hart Westlake was
a work colleague and Griffin Meyer a family friend. The latter two were married, their
wives in attendance.

Kento attended to some work via his phone.
Numbers were just coming in on the Fastracc
revenues, and they were even better than he
expected. The staff had worked hard on the
project, and he authorized a salary bonus to
the team.

"What's with the rabbit food?" Hart chided
when Suni brought in their lunch.

"These are foods for high energy. Here at
Locklear Lodge, we want to do everything
we can to foster the participants' well-being
on wedding day. There's a spinach salad with

avocado, walnuts and dried goji berries. And grilled chicken breast. All energy-boosters."

"Hey, Suni," Demarcus chimed in, "how about some double bacon cheeseburgers? That'll give us plenty of pep."

She raised her eyebrows at him in a good-natured way. "Dark chocolate to finish with and green tea to drink."

Hart pitched, "How about some cold beers?"

Even mild-mannered Griffin joined the fun with, "And a nap. A nice long nap would give us loads of vim and vigor."

"I can't promise a nap—" Suni shrugged "—but you can have whatever you want to eat and drink after the ceremony."

Kento smiled at their carrying on, but his mind was elsewhere.

"What's up?" Lucas noticed Kento's pensiveness as the others helped themselves to the food. The two had formed a strong bond in high school and university years and kept in touch, but with calls and texts that became less frequent as time went on. It was an honor that Lucas had asked him to stand at his side when he married his beloved. "Everything right with you and Erin? You hadn't even told me that you two were in communication."

"Absolutely right." He forced a bright answer.

Things were actually a little *too* right with her. That was the problem. He didn't like how the combination of blazing lovemaking and the *forever after* sentiments of this wedding were making him feel. They were causing him to second-guess. And that was not something he did. Kento was a man of conviction. That's how he built his empire. He never put out a product before it was ready. Never made a miscalculation. Never regretted hiring or firing an employee. Just the same, he'd gotten on the plane to Seattle with the certainty that relationships, and definitely marriage, would never, ever be in his future.

Finding that Erin hadn't betrayed him in the way he'd always assumed she had, his brain short-circuited while it tried to sort true from false, impossibility from opportunity, head from heart. While the tailor attended to Lucas's tux, Kento stared at himself in one of the full-length mirrors. What was on Erin's mind right now while she got glammed up with the girls? Was she thinking about him?

This time Mr. Sure of Himself was anything but.

* * *

The best man and maid of honor strode toward the altar. While doing so, Erin forgot for the tiniest moment again that she was wearing a shocking violet gown and not a white one. That the guests assembled had not brought the toasters and china place settings for her. That the breathtaking man whose arm she was holding wasn't about to become her mate. *Husband* suddenly sounded like the sweetest word she had ever heard, and yearning flooded through her.

As they had rehearsed, they moved in measured increments. Instead of a fabric runner, the aisle they walked down was delineated by a carpet of moss that was pretty but actually not that easy to navigate. Erin's heels kept getting tangled every few steps, and Kento had to disguise his little tugs that helped her from falling and being ensnared by the greenery. They moved on pace toward the archway altar that was now completely covered in cascading wisteria. She'd figured that with Seattle's frequent rain they'd use a marquee tent for shelter, but instead it was a dry day and it had been decided that the ceremony could be held in the open air. There were clouds, but sunlight peeked through them. A flutist played from a nearby bench. Guests sat on both sides of the aisle, on rows of white chairs dressed with white cushions in the center of the extensive lawn, the lodge's forest of trees behind the altar framing the space.

When they reached the arch, Kento and Erin parted toward their respective sides. An involuntary wince shot through her after separating herself from him. It was wrong that she was starting to like being with him more than being without him, and she knew it. Those inclinations could only lead to more agony, and hadn't the two of them suffered enough by each other's doings?

The bride and her enormous dress, with a skirt full enough to house four small children under it, minced slowly up the aisle, accompanied by her father. Now standing next to the three bridesmaids, Erin reflected as she watched Christy approach. All that had happened with Kento still felt unresolved— many misunderstandings, many mistakes made. And most significantly, both of them wore so many scars from the past they'd been completely disfigured by them. Even if she thought she could open up to something ongoing with him again, to try to heal, he'd made it abundantly clear that he couldn't. Glancing over, she noticed her mother seated in one of the rows of chairs, talking to someone Erin couldn't see due to the tall woman with a big hat who sat in front of her.

With Lucas beaming, Christy detached from her father and joined her groom to face the wedding officiant. Erin took the bride's bouquet as had been rehearsed.

They were just not meant to be, her and Kento. She had to accept it. Maybe in another lifetime, not this one. She knew that she should take charge of the situation by not making it any worse, not getting any closer. Under no circumstances should she make love with him again. It had been too perfect, too moving, too life-affirming. The least she could do is spare them getting any further invested in each other, which would make tomorrow's separation even more harrowing.

"Ladies and gentlemen, we are gathered here today to celebrate the union of Christy and Lucas," the officiant began.

The ceremony progressed quickly. Or was it that Erin's focus drifted in and out from the long rhyming poem written and read by an older uncle of Lucas's?

This day begins our start, in the waters we shall chart
Holding hands we now depart, as I keep you in my heart
You are my work of art, sharing wisdom we impart
If we fight we will restart, we must be smart, for life is sweet but sometimes tart
May we never be apart, for you are my...
counterpart.

Christy dabbed away a tear.

Erin glanced over to Kento, who closed his eyes and mimicked his head dropping sideways as if he had fallen asleep, making it hard for her not to laugh.

The conventional vows were spoken, and soon enough Erin was reunited with Kento's arm, firm and strong, and they receded down the aisle.

Guests were directed to the grand ballroom inside the lodge for the reception. There was a photo call for the bridal party, as Christy had gone the traditional route of not letting

Lucas see her in her dress until she walked down the aisle. They were sequestered in an area prepared for the task, with all sorts of flower arrangements on pedestals set against the backdrop of tall green trees.

Suni assisted the photographer with his groupings.

"When do we get to eat?" Kento whispered into Erin's ear. "Did you have those salads when you were getting dressed? Nice, but I'm starved."

"I can't eat until the photos are done. It might muss up my lipstick."

"*I'd* like to muss up your lipstick," Kento let fly. The electric thrill that shot through Erin's body was a charge that could have lit up Seattle. He needed to stop being so unrelentingly sexy. A girl could only take so much.

She forced out what she wanted to say, though with limited conviction. "I don't think we should do any more…mussing, if you know what I mean. You're leaving tomorrow, and we've gone far past the playacting we agreed to participate in."

"Oh, that's right, we were supposed to be pretending, weren't we?" he responded with a bitter sort of undertone she didn't exactly understand.

"I mean, we've both made it clear we have no interest in relationships. Especially after our past together. But my plan may have backfired." She saw no reason not to be honest with him again. "The more time we spend with each other, the more I question..."

"Okay, I'll need everyone lined up for a group shot," the photographer called.

Wasn't Kento feeling the same thing—that every second they were together was going to make it harder and harder for him to board that plane? She was willing to state that out loud. How would withholding words serve her at this point? She might have thought she could pull off this charade, but she'd underestimated the influence Kento still had over her. And it had become impossible to distinguish what was real and what was fantasy. She was dreading having to say goodbye so soon tomorrow. Although it was for the best.

With the photos finally completed, everyone except the bride and groom, who would be formally announced as a married couple, was seen into the ballroom.

With smiles left and right, the best man

and maid of honor said hello to many of the guests in the large ballroom. Hors d'oeuvres were passed on trays held by waiters in white jackets. Erin had one of each of the chicken satay skewers with peanut sauce, spinach and feta cheese meatballs, and crostini with olive tapenade that had been refined yesterday to the bride's satisfaction. All were delicious. Marionberry spritzers were pretty and frosty cold.

The ballroom was done up to Christy and Aunt Olivia's exact specifications. Tables were dressed in dark green linen. Lavender-colored napkins were rolled and tied with twine into which a sprig of wisteria was slipped. The china was copper-rimmed. Centerpieces were enormous on tall pedestals, with larkspur, lilac and hydrangea selections dotted with long strands of fairy lights.

Out of the corner of her eye, Erin spotted her mother in conversation with a man she could only see from the back. Recognizing immediately who it was, apprehension darkened over her like a raincloud. Without drawing Kento's attention, she said to a woman she was chatting with, "Excuse me for a minute."

While he continued his conversation with

some of the guests, she beelined across the room toward her mother, where her suspicion was confirmed. Important business in Walla Walla was supposed to have been so critical it was going to keep Ingram Barclay from attending the wedding. Yet there he was in a tuxedo and tailcoat. "Father, why are you here?"

"Your mother called me, and rightly so. I flew into town and chartered a ferry to the island." Erin glared at Bunny, whose face pinched as she listened to her husband. "Surely you don't think we're going to allow you to get involved again with Kento Yama-moto."

With the band having taken the stage, the reception was in full swing. Oldies dance songs had many revelers up and boogying in the grand ballroom, another event space on the lodge's property with walls built mainly from glass to display the lush flora outside, a formal garden filled with fountains, birdbaths and colorful flowers. Bridesmaid Amber caught Kento's eye as he watched her literally drag groomsman Demarcus onto the dance floor, the poor guy popping the crostini he held in his hand right into his mouth to keep up. She wore that same brash violet color as Erin and the other bridesmaids. He didn't know where the maid of honor had gone, but he was ready for her return. This whole wedding biz was much easier to take with her on his arm.

In his bed, too, but that was another matter entirely. In fact, he'd been thinking during the ceremony that as magnificent as it was to make glorious love with Erin last night, the long-dormant passion in him set aflame, she was right to say up front that she didn't think they should do it again. Even with the past hurts from the Barclays explained, the calculated ambitions of Ayaka behind him and the childhood of rejection now history, Kento made it his policy to keep his guard up at all times. His armor was always on. He wasn't a man who was ever going to rely on anyone. But instead of confirming those edicts, as was his intention this weekend, Erin made him question them. Things were becoming too dangerous—*she* was too dangerous. What he felt around her could explode his plan into a million pieces.

He wholeheartedly alleged that trust was

what fed an intimate relationship, which would shrivel and dry up without it. Good for Lucas and Christy, he'd thought as they promised each other love and loyalty at the altar. Of course, the *for richer or for poorer* part of the vows sounded silly coming out of the mouths of Seattle's bluebloods, where daughters were still bargained off along like land and holdings. Erin would walk down the wedding aisle to her approved future someday, and it wasn't going to be Kento. A part of him wished he could steal her away to be his, to take her back to Japan where she could leave this life that wasn't making her happy, anyway.

After the band finished the song they were playing, the ballroom lights flashed and then went slightly dim. The bandleader, a stocky man whose limbs strained against his tuxedo, boomed through his microphone, "Introducing for the first time as husband and wife, Mr. and Mrs. Lucas Collins."

A purple-tinged spotlight was aimed at the ballroom's entrance as Lucas and Christy burst in holding hands. At the same time, Erin arrived at Kento's side. The band began the song that would be the couple's first dance.

As they took to the dance floor, the videographer and photographer snaked in a circle around them, capturing the moment.

Kento noticed there was a stress in Erin's eyes, her brows slightly bunched, that hadn't been there before. While they watched the newlyweds, he asked, "Is everything okay?"

He could tell she was making a decision before she told him, "My father is here."

"And that bothers you?"

"He wasn't expected to come. My mother called to tell him you and I had resparked our romance."

Understanding why she was upset, his own blood pressure rose. He'd hoped not to get involved in any conversation with either of Erin's parents other than to exchange pleasantries. No longer the intimidated twenty-one-year-old, Kento saw no benefit in cutting loose the fury he'd held for the Barclays. It was of no importance now—he just wanted to get through the weekend and get back home. There was nothing to be gained by any kind of confrontation with them. That was Erin's fight, should she ever suit up and make it to the battle line.

After the bride danced with her father

and then father-in-law, the groom with his mother-in-law and then with his own mother, the bandleader announced, "We now call for the best man and maid of honor."

Kento firmly grasped Erin's hand and led her to the center of the dance floor. He pulled her close and they began to sway. Once they'd reached a rhythm, he asked into her ear, "Did your father have anything new to say on the topic?"

"I told him that I had maid of honor responsibilities and that we needed to discuss it later."

"What is there to talk about?"

"I'll have to explain that us getting back together is a hoax."

The sequence of lies and exposures had gotten complicated, just as he'd suspected it might. "Which means you'll have to tell your parents that one of the main reasons you embarked on this charade is because of your mother trying to fix you up with every society billionaire in Seattle. Even though ending up with one of them is, actually, the destiny you're allowing them to choose for you."

They whirled to the music, photos and video capturing every move. Kento felt him-

self becoming more and more agitated. For
her, but maybe for himself as well. Because
perhaps he had to admit that he secretly did
want to see where this weekend with Erin
might lead. Could it be that she'd hammered
cracks into his stone wall? Was it possible
that he might he be able to open his heart
after all? He'd become a man who got what
he wanted. What was it he wanted this time?
In any case, he wished that the options were
not her parents' but his and Erin's.

"I suppose a few years from now I'll hear
through Lucas that you produced a couple
of heirs to the throne," he egged her on. He
felt her body freeze in response. She stopped
dancing, forcing him to stop as well. With
a smile so fake she could be a model in a
toothpaste commercial, she moved to leave
the dance floor.

His jaw pulsed, him exasperated by his
own lack of diplomacy, conceding that this
was further proof that he was not meant to get
close to someone. She must have already been
upset that her father found it necessary to fly
in to intercede. Kento had made it worse by
not controlling his own reaction. He grabbed

her hand before she could scoot away. "I'm sorry. I shouldn't have said that."

"It's what you think."

"That may be true, but what kind of bully am I? I'm as bad as your parents." His strong impulses toward her were making him desperate. How could he argue with her family allegiance when that was a value he respected? "It's not right that I made you feel judged. That's something I know far too much about myself."

"We sure spend a lot of time apologizing to each other, don't we?" she asked with a half smile.

"Let's eat."

As they sat down to dinner, the first course was served: Alaskan king crab cakes. With Erin sitting at Christy's side and Kento next to Lucas, they didn't talk after that sharp exchange on the dance floor. He spotted Ingram and Bunny a few tables away. If either of them cared to engage in a stare down, he was more than ready. But, of course, they were too cowardly to give him more than an occasional glance.

In accepting Lucas's request for him to stand as best man, Kento had figured he'd be encountering both of Erin's parents. What he hadn't expected was discovering all of the new information that brought the musing about Erin he'd been haunted by in Tokyo into a different light. Which made her predicament a frustration he himself experienced along with her, for her. At this point, getting back on that plane to the place that was now home couldn't come soon enough. Although his suitcase full of thoughts about Erin was going to be heavier, not lighter.

After the entrée of beef Wellington and crispy brussels sprouts, the time for the maid of honor and best man's most important task of the night arrived. She was to speak first, and then his speech would be a champagne toast as wedding cake was served.

Erin stood and was handed a mic. She spoke of the serene location and how nice the ceremony was. Wished the couple every happiness and then looked over to Kento, whom she hadn't spoken with during the meal. "Earlier, I was reviewing my speech and decided I wanted to find a quotation that was meaningful to me personally, as a gift I could give to Christy and Lucas." The bride and groom kissed, and the guests applauded them doing so. Erin focused her eyes on Kento's and kept them there as she finished. "Sophocles tells us that 'one word frees us of all the weight and pain of life. That word is *love*.'"

The message bulleted into Kento, making his Adam's apple twitch. He couldn't help thinking those were words she'd picked for him, not the newlyweds. He'd heard sentiments to that effect before, yet they'd never sounded as poignant. Could love set them free?

The mic was passed. It was his turn. He began, "As some of you know, I live in Tokyo. So I thought I'd bring along some age-old wisdom from Japanese proverbs. The first is 'Eat before falling in love.'" Laughter came from various directions. "I presume what the ancients meant by that is that love is all-encompassing and can command your full attention. Love is hard work. It's not for the weak." More chuckles came as a response. As the champagne was poured, he offered his well wishes to the happy couple.

As Kento lifted his glass high, the guests followed suit. His eyes met Erin's; she hadn't taken hers off him. In fact, her stare bored into him. "And I'll conclude with another Japanese proverb that says simply, 'No road is too long in the company of a friend.'"

Erin bit her lip as her eyes became glassy. Kento sat down.

The cake was wheeled across the dance floor. It was a three-tiered white affair with green frosting trees decorating the sides. No doubt a tribute to the Pacific Northwest but a bit tacky, in his opinion. Slices were soon delivered to each place setting, and coffee service followed immediately after.

At a discreet moment, Kento got up and moved behind Christy and Lucas to Erin's chair. He leaned down and hushed into her ear, "We've done our job. Let's get out of here."

She turned her head toward him in question. "What do you mean?"

"It's early. Let's go into the city. I've got a boat for us."

CHAPTER SEVEN

"WHEN DID YOU arrange this?" Erin asked as Kento helped her into the limousine waiting at the lodge's main entrance. He took a seat beside her, allowing the driver to then close the door.

"During the beef Wellington. After I was such a jerk to you on the dance floor." Being teased about her station in life and fidelity to her parents—as she viewed it, anyway—was no joking matter. He'd become aggravated at Ingram's arrival as well. And wished he could do something to protect her. From her own parents? That was family drama he had no place in. Making a joke about sometime down the line hearing from Lucas that Erin had produced the heirs everyone was waiting for was a low blow he wished hadn't snapped out of his mouth.

"What's this?" she asked as he slid over a

large gift bag from the floor of the limo. It was gold with two handles, and the contents were hidden by bunches of shimmery tissue paper.

"Just something I had the driver pick up from a personal shopper."

After a quizzical look, she yanked at the tissue, throwing it left and right, which gave him a grin. As intended, the item she pulled out was a tan-colored woolen coat.

"I stole you away from the wedding. The least I could do is keep you warm."

"Just as you gave me your jacket when we walked together after the welcome dinner." She shook her head in charmed disbelief, her smile filling him with delight. "Where are we headed?"

There was a double meaning to that question.

"Let's revisit somewhere we used to go."

The limo delivered them to the island harbor. Kento ushered her into a private ferry he'd ordered online from his phone, which he'd cleverly hidden under the table during dinner. He'd guessed her size closely enough that the coat fit her well. After the short ride to the city dock, another limo met them there.

Once they were ensconced inside, he pulled a bottle of champagne from the silver ice bucket it rested in and poured some into the crystal flutes provided on a tray.

"To history." He lifted his glass.

"One word frees us of all the weight and pain of life. That word is love.*"*

He didn't know why he was toasting their sometimes painful past, only that it was something they were bound by. Shared. Together. It was genuine. Before extortions, bent realities and inevitability tore them apart, they'd passed far more good times together than bad. She was still the only woman who had affected his soul.

With that, after they clinked glasses and sipped, he leaned right over and planted a deep kiss onto her sweet lips. Their tongues met in an intermingling that sent pleasure down his entire body. His fingers threaded through the silk of her hair as he held her head to him. One kiss led to another in a dreamy haze that he couldn't break away from.

"Excuse me, sir," the voice of the limo driver came in through the speaker. "Would you like me to continue driving without a destination?"

Erin giggled, and then so did Kento. "We weren't supposed to do that anymore," he scolded her, wagging his finger like a disapproving schoolteacher. "You are too alluring!" Her sly smile in return made his chest swell.

"Do you want to do something goofy like go to the Space Needle?" she suggested.

Raising his glass to tap hers again, he instructed the driver to take them there.

Memories flooded him when they reached the Seattle Center, where several of the city's tourist attractions were located. He recalled countless times that he and Erin would lie on a blanket on one of the many patches of lawn that surrounded the Needle. The driver let them out at the entrance base. Both of them tilted their heads back to look upward at the impressive height of the tower from this vantage point.

"We going up?"

"Absolutely," she answered. "I never do tourist things."

"And I feel like a visitor in my hometown."

He bought tickets, and they were soon in

the elevator rocketing them over six hundred feet upward to the observation decks.

Since the last time Kento had visited, much had been changed at the top of the Needle, including a revolving glass floor. "It's always been an unbeatable view," he mused aloud as he and Erin made their way around the circular deck that afforded vistas from all angles. At one point they stopped to stare silently at the cityscape, sparkling in the night sky. Without knowing if his hand reached for hers or hers for his, suddenly her velvety palm was in his grasp.

Kento had seen the world's sights from the sky, from atop the Empire State Building to the Eiffel Tower to Dubai's Burj Khalifa. Yet there was nothing like this. Because Erin was next to him. "Did you know that the initial design for the Space Needle was sketched on a napkin by a hotelier?" she asked.

"Yeah. That story was always inspiring to me. Remember how many times we used to hang out here lying on the lawn?"

They'd come to study, to relax, to kiss, to talk.

"I used to bring one of those blankets with the university logo printed all over it." After spreading it open, she'd stretch out on her back, body flat to the ground. And he'd lie down as well, perpendicular, with his head on her stomach, where he'd stare idly at this space-age architectural marvel, the flying saucer in the sky.

During those quiet times, when she'd rhythmically comb her fingers through his hair seemingly for hours on end, he'd felt completely accepted. All of the negative talk and ridicule, and sometimes humiliation, of his upbringing would disappear. The worn shoes on his feet when everybody else had a new pair each season didn't matter. All the sneers of Erin's sorority sisters and her parents held nothing over him in those moments.

"In a way, those afternoons here with you were when I had the inklings of what would be my first software design." Which launched his empire. It occurred to him, for the first time, how much he owed her for that approval. For that safe space. Without it, he wasn't sure he'd be in the position he was. The enemies might have beaten him down after all. "We had something pretty great once, didn't we?" he asked wistfully, both of them still looking out at the city.

"When I was with you, I almost believed I could have anything I wanted."

"What would you want if there was nothing holding you back?"

"Are you really asking?"

"I don't pose questions if I'm not interested in the answer."

"I'll show you when we're done here."

After the elevator delivered them back to terra firma, they returned to the limo. Erin called up an address on her phone and instructed the driver. Kento was intrigued.

A bit later, the driver pulled to the curb of a mansion in the city's Queen Anne neighborhood.

"What are we looking at?"

"You asked what I'd do if I could do anything. I'd buy this mansion. That's what I'd like to pursue, acquiring historic properties. Find the really special ones. Faithfully restore them if they need it. Research chandeliers and woodwork and all the details."

"That's what Barclay Properties does. Your parents and your paternal grandparents."

"Yes, but they give me reports to check, a bunch of numbers our accountants have already prepared. Or an office task, such as pricing new computers for employees. They're just marking time until they can marry me off."

"Erin, this isn't the olden days. You can have a meaningful career and still produce children."

"Tell that to them."

"Have *you*?"

"Yes. They don't listen."

"Do you ever think of just…breaking away?"

"Of course. But where would I go? Alone." His heart cracked for her. At how little choice she perceived herself to have. "You were the only taste of independence I've ever had. You encouraged me to think and say anything I wanted to."

"We gave each other more than we realized at the time."

"I wish it wasn't too late."

"Is it?" What was he thinking? That there was some scenario that saw the two of them together after tomorrow? It was impossible, yet he couldn't conceive of walking away from her again. Was it too much to dream of more? He owned a private jet and had every resource money could buy at his disposal.

Perhaps he could start by returning to Seattle again in a few weeks. Maybe every few weeks. Alternately, he could fly her to him if she'd come.

While he'd been so convinced an ongoing union wasn't for him, spending time with Erin had made him doubt those conclusions. Could he leave the hurt behind and start a future with her? And even if he could, what about her? She was resigned to her lot, considered it her destiny. But maybe they could start slowly and get more acquainted with the adults they'd become rather than just debriefing on the past. Perhaps, in time, he could help her see her options in a new light.

"What do you like about this property?" He decided to start getting to know her better right now.

"I've toured it. Built in 1902. Ten thousand square feet. What I love—" she gestured as she spoke "—is the wraparound terraces with marble tile flooring and fantastic views. And look at those double entrance doors."

"Do you know a lot about real estate?"

"Not formally. But it's in my blood, I guess. Is it interesting to you?"

"What's interesting to *you* is what's interesting to me. Tell me more."

"It's three stories with curved wooden staircases. A massive party lounge with a built-in wooden bar. A full catering kitchen. Twenty-three original chandeliers."

Her enthusiasm was infectious. He couldn't help but lean in and swoop a kiss to her cheek. The chuckle he got in return was enchanting. After she'd shown him another property she liked in Ballard, the limo driver asked through the speaker where they wanted to go next. "Just go ahead and circle the city," Kento answered. With the privacy glass separating them from the driver and the blackout windows of the limo allowing them to look out but no one to see in, Kento knew exactly the sights he wanted to take in next.

Leaning over, he brought a hand to Erin's face and then kissed her other cheek with its creamy softness. His mouth found hers, and he kissed her intensely, a ravenous kiss that felt like a man's daily bread, like something he couldn't live without. When he'd had enough to survive for a minute, he moved down to her throat. The catch of desire he heard in her breath encouraged him on. Warm enough in the heated limo, he slid the coat he'd bought her off, first one silken shoulder and then the other.

To think, it had only been a few hours ago when she marched down the wedding aisle in that violet gown she still wore. The one he was reaching behind her to unzip. He shimmied it down her body and off her and made short work of the lingerie underneath. Likewise, he slipped off her shoes. There she was for him, completely naked, gorgeous, excitement evident in her eyes. He sat back and pulled her onto his lap, him still in his tuxedo because he wanted to slowly caress and savor every inch of her before undressing.

He poured a fresh flute of champagne and brought it to her lips for a sip. And took one himself from the exact same spot her mouth had touched. Just to provoke her response, he brought the cold flute to the skin of her neck. The tip of her tongue darted out to flick her upper lip in arousal. His teeth bared with pleasure, his loins bracing under his trousers. He drizzled a bit of the champagne onto her exposed throat only so that he could quickly lick it off. Her head fell back at the same time her spine arched to allow him even greater access.

Eventually, with an occasional glance through the blackout windows to the downtown office buildings, he laid Erin down on the limo seat. After removing a condom from his wallet, he stripped off his tuxedo and got on top of her. The elevation to which they brought each other was far higher than the top of the Space Needle they'd just come down from.

"Where to now?" After the urgent merging of body and soul that Erin and Kento had just shared in the limo, she wasn't ready to return to the wedding across the Sound at the lodge. No doubt a group of drunken revelers were still dancing, now to recorded music once the band finished. She most certainly didn't want to encounter her parents. That could wait until tomorrow. Her mother calling her father in from out of town was yet another indignity Erin would have to add to her already full mental tote bag of similar behavior.

No, she didn't want to think about any of that at the moment. All she could see, breathe, feel or hear was the naked man sprawled right next to her, who was stroking her cheek with the backs of his fingers. After the fiasco with Harris, she thought she'd arrive at the wedding with a hardened heart and not susceptible to any new, or revisited, emotions. She'd greatly underestimated the magical powers of Kento Yamamoto to make her care, to make her hope, to make her imagine.

"Are any of those nightclubs we used to go to still around?" he suggested. With Seattle the birthplace of many great musicians, the city's live music scene was a mecca. There had been countless nights that she and Kento spent nursing a long-necked beer bottle and listening to a rock-and-roll band, some good, some simply loud.

"That's not something I ever do anymore, either, but let's look it up." With a few swipes on her phone, she located a club that sounded promising and gave the driver the address. They crawled back into their clothes, Kento in his tux again but skipping the tie. Despite their agreement that they shouldn't further complicate the weekend with more physical intimacy, their pull toward each other had trampled over any common sense.

People milled about outside the Emerald

Bar. Dressed in jeans, flannel and leather, it looked to be a crowd of university students. Just as they once were. Which made her so aware of how much time had moved on. All heads shot toward them when the limo pulled up to the curb. Eschewing the driver's offer to open the door for them, Kento exited and extended his arm to Erin to help her out.

"I just thought of the fact that tuxedo and gown isn't quite the dress code for places like this," she said, hearing the thumping music spilling out from the club's doors.

"I suppose not," he replied with a chuckle.

They were eyed up and down by the people outside, where there was nothing for Erin and Kento to do but shrug their shoulders. A girl with arms covered in tattoos called good-naturedly, "How was the wedding?"

"Pretty good," Kento answered for them, "but our personal after-party was even better."

Erin sparkled recalling the drive around Seattle they'd just taken, the limo serving as more than just a mode of transportation. She forked a hand through her hair, wondering if it had become messy, although not really caring if she looked wanton. On the arm of the most appealing man she had ever known and after what they just did, she felt confident in her own sexuality in a way she never had before as they traipsed into the club.

Finding seats to the side of the stage, he pulled out the chair for her to sit and then arranged his own to be right next to it. The small table was wood and people had carved their initials or slogans into it. "Beer?" he asked above the beat of the band as he perused the sticky laminated menu card, noting that even in a dive like this the brews were artisanal with lofty descriptions. That was Seattle. "How about notes of pine, herbs and orange peel with a bitter crispy finish?"

Which struck them both as funny. "How can beer be crispy?" she inquired.

He mimicked taking a big bite and ordered two when the waitress came.

Soon they were sipping from long-necked bottles, just like the old days, as they both pumped their shoulders in rhythm with the bass-heavy foursome on stage. All skinny in torn jeans, two with bushy beards, the band blasted out rapid-fire songs one after the next.

Erin surely couldn't remember the last time

she'd had this much fun. Why couldn't have things gone differently for them? her mind lamented. All these years when she'd thought of him, it was with the sting of loss, of being walked out on. Knowing now that he thought she was part of the militia mustered to force him out only slightly assuaged that mixed-up ache.

What if he had told her about the bribes and threats? Would she have stayed with him, taken a side? If she was being brutally honest, probably not. She would have been too afraid back then. But in her imagination, what if she had chosen him over her parents? Might they have gone forward as young adults together in Seattle? Would he have stayed here, or would he have pursued the opportunity with his uncle in Tokyo, anyway?

The central question that had arisen time and time again lit up in her mind like it was written in neon lights. If he'd asked her to move to Japan with him, would she have? Might not that have been her only chance at a true break from the preplanned life her parents had already drafted for her?

Five thousand miles could have been far enough away, on a continent they had no connection to, for them to give up on running her life. Would they have let her be out of spite, daring her to turn her back on their money and the safety it brought? Or would they have chased after her, employing surveillance, making her life unpleasant and still controlled? She was only beginning to understand the depths of their cold-bloodedness, so maybe it was a naive fantasy to think she could have jetted away with Kento from everything she knew, to start fresh. But it was a dream she'd allowed herself for seven long years.

After two sets from the band and two crispy beers, they were hungry. Returning to the still-in-business twenty-four-hour diner they used to go to for late-night eats, they sauntered in with their violet satin and black tux. The decor had been spruced up, but the vibe was the same. Night-crawling hipsters, workers who'd just finished shifts, lovers who only had eyes for each other, even big family groups all munched from massive, heavy white plates. Kento and Erin ordered breakfast food of bacon and eggs, served with potatoes, toast and coffee. They dug in as soon as it was served.

She returned to the thoughts of what could have been that she'd had at the club. And the far recess of her mind was screaming, *What about now?* She didn't know whether to give that voice any credence, yet it kept popping up. With fork in hand, she asked, "Tell me more about your life in Tokyo. How did you go from working for your uncle to creating NIRE?"

"It's a fast pace there in general, but I have to admit I ascended quickly. I was just ahead of the curve on what people wanted programs to do for them. I seem to have a knack for coming up with what the market will respond to."

"So, as soon as you got there, you started working at your uncle's office?"

"Yeah, at first I lived with some other cousins on the outskirts of town and had to commute into the city every day. Uncle Riku had a small development company, and I did coding for him and whatever work he needed done. I started designing apps in my spare time. After I sold the first few, I got on to the big software projects I had in mind, and I had enough money to open my own office."

Erin tried to picture that. Going to look at

empty office space to lease in the modern high-rise buildings of the business districts. Attending to all of the details of running a business. She was amazed at his bravery, still only in his midtwenties when this was taking shape. Opening his own company had to have been a big risk to take. "Did you hire employees right away?"

"We started with a small staff in a space that had one office and a half dozen workstations. Within a couple of years, we took over the entire floor. Now we have six floors and a think tank outside the city."

"Was it ever an obstacle for you, being an American?" What she was really asking was how it would have been for *her* had she gone with him. Which, of course, wasn't a true comparison, as he was of Japanese descent and spoke the language.

"The culture is more formal and modest there than it is here. People don't express how they feel as much. And they don't touch as casually. They bow. Social hierarchies are important."

How would she have fared as a stranger in a strange land? Learning any language was a challenge, but Japanese, with its character sets and writing systems, would have been especially difficult. Not looking like the majority, when walking down the street she'd have been instantly identified as a foreigner. In addition to language, there were those social norms to learn. Could she have made a life there, created a home for the two of them?

"Where do you live?"

"Now that's just like it would be anywhere in the world for a bachelor billionaire. I have a sleek penthouse on the forty-third floor. Glass walls, black and chrome furniture, extra rooms I never use. Food delivered. A housekeeper who takes care of everything. I'm a cliché." Erin tried to picture what he was describing—an elevator like the Space Needle's shooting him up to his apartment. He abruptly put down his fork and reached across the table to take both of Erin's hands in his. "Why don't you come visit me sometime and let me show you?"

After their explosive encounter under the shower and in his cabin last night, they'd agreed not to make love again, that they'd stop playing with fire. Which was supposed to help keep her internal volcano from erupting. But they hadn't held themselves back.

Tonight, being in the city with him again had switched the light inside her to the on position. From this evening forward, she was forever changed. In fact, she knew in a blink that she was going to see that penthouse, lie down on his bed in the sky. No matter what it took.

"I don't speak a word of Japanese."

"You could learn."

"Teach me how to say something. Right now."

"Okay." He hesitated then said, looking into her waiting eyes, *"Aishiteru."*

"What does that mean?"

"It means 'I love you.'"

After the ferry whisked Erin and Kento back across the Sound in the wee hours, they returned to his cabin. Due in the morning at the gift-opening brunch, in a few hours they would be thrown right back into the throng of the wedding party. It had been a long day, and after a dozen or so tender kisses goodnight in bed, beautiful Erin fell quickly to sleep in his arms.

Slumber didn't come as easily for him as he watched the night shadows play against the skylight in the bedroom.

Aishiteru.

I love you.

He'd said it aloud. In two languages. The crazy thing was, it was true. It had always been true. Maybe the stars had been in his favor when Erin had the idea of a fake boyfriend for the weekend. Without that, they wouldn't have spent so much time together, helping him to realize that it wasn't the past with her he planned to forget that mattered. It was the future they were going to create.

He stroked her arm ever so gently so as not to wake her, the mild movement in contrast to the giddiness inside him. He'd declared his love to a woman. To *the* woman that he'd been in love with all along. How distorted a mind could get five thousand miles away from the person who owned his heart. Pain had removed the longings of his soul.

When he'd uttered those important words in two different tongues, she didn't return them. For a moment, sitting in the diner's orange plastic booth, their plates of American breakfast in front of them, he'd felt slapped by her lack of response. Fortunately, the practicality and patience that had enabled him to build his company to where it was today served him in this facet of life also.

He'd wounded her so critically years ago. Even though he was only a frightened kid, he'd always been tormented by guilt that he'd deserted her in the process. And learning this weekend about how little she knew of what went on made him guiltier still. After him, she'd had a series of disappointments in dating. Then she was abandoned, another dismissal, by Harris. She was quite smart not to bark out a forced and cursory *I love you, too*.

The moon shining in from the skylight above his bed shifted to give a glow to her face. He could wait for her. In a way, he'd been waiting for her all along. They'd go at her pace. He had to earn her trust again, and that was okay with him. The main thing was that they'd made a plan at the diner. He'd return to Seattle in a few weeks. After that, she'd agreed to come to Japan. She'd even expressed interest in learning about the customs that she would be unfamiliar with. It wouldn't be easy there as a white woman without knowing the language. They'd start by getting a tutor here. Optimism tingled through him. He wouldn't just show her Tokyo, but he'd take her outside the city, to see stunning Mount Fuji. Like Mount Rainier here in Washington, Fuji was the tallest volcano in the area. There were so many places he wanted to show her in the beautiful country he called home.

Above all else, Erin was finally determined to chart her own path. That would be far harder for her than learning a new language. The break she'd have to make from her parents might be absolute. That they could hate Kento enough to turn their back on their daughter was in and of itself an illustration of their character, one that should make it easier for her to walk away. He could support her as much as possible, but that turning point would be hers alone. Dotting her peaceful-looking face with wispy kisses, he knew she could tackle whatever lay ahead. It was her time.

His eyes moved to the dream catcher party favor the guests had been given at the rehearsal dinner. He lifted it from the nightstand and hooked it onto the bedpost. It must be working, he thought with a smile that no one saw. Holding Erin, he finally drifted into a contented sleep.

At daybreak, Erin left his embrace to go prepare for the morning. They'd meet at the brunch. But when Kento arrived to the lodge's lounge, he couldn't spot her anywhere. Christy and Lucas were front and center, with the guests seated at small tables arranged in a semicircle around them. People nibbled from their brunch plates—baked French toast, a fruit and yogurt bar, and coffee and tea were set up as a buffet. Lucas held up the latest kitchen mixer, eliciting oohs and wows from the group. Christy tore the silver wrapping paper from a set of luxury bedsheets.

He spotted Amber and Demarcus sitting together, his arm around the bridesmaid. *Good*, Kento thought, suddenly soppy about people finding their significant other. As a matter of fact, on closer survey, he also saw MacKenzie and Divya each sitting with a man. Bunny and Ingram were nowhere to be found.

Kento was beginning to get worried about Erin and stepped out of the lounge to call her. Until his eye caught sight of Ingram in a small side salon across the lobby. Kento made his way over there, wondering if Erin was with him.

Careful not to be seen, as she needed to

deal with her parents herself, he got close enough to see that Bunny and Erin were in the room as well, huddled close. All three of their faces were strained. Still moving sideways to avoid notice, Kento couldn't help but listen in when he heard the harsh tones coming from their mouths.

"It started out fake, but it's become real. Realer than anything I've ever felt."

"We won't stand for it."

"You should like Kento now, Father," Erin hissed. "He has both fame and fortune. Lots and lots of money. Let's order the criteria of what's important to you. Is there anything besides pedigree and wealth?"

"Erin, are we to have a repeat of seven years ago?" Ingram asked sternly.

Bunny followed suit. "He's not one of our kind."

"What on earth does that even mean anymore? Isn't rich and successful *our* kind of people? I found someone rich."

Kento winced. She'd *found* someone rich. He didn't like the sound of that. Why didn't she say that she'd *found* someone she loved? Oh, that's right, she'd never told him that she loved him. Last night during the fun and exhilaration of the limo and the nightclub, she'd confided a change, but not one she was honestly going to be able to make. Maybe it was something that sounded doable in theory but, when push came to shove, she couldn't put it into practice.

"For heaven's sake, Erin," her father scolded. "You know what your mother means. Established families. Multigenerational wealth. You have a duty to marry strategically and produce the next generation of the Barclay legacy."

Erin glared at both of them but had no retort. Here it was. In the time it took for the wedding guests to spoon blueberry yogurt into their mouths, Kento's dream come true had morphed into the recurring nightmare from the past. She wasn't going to stand up to them. Ever. He recognized the body language. Her shoulders slumped. Her eyes deadened. Once again, she'd been defeated.

Unable to witness any longer, Kento dashed away. As he rushed toward his cabin, cries of disappointment stifled in his throat. How ridiculous of him to allow the thoughts he'd had while lying in bed a few dark hours ago with Erin warm against his chest. He should have been the wiser one at the diner, where they talked like they had as young adults about great plans and bright days ahead.

He burst into his cabin and slammed the door shut. Furious with himself. Why didn't he protect her from fighting a futile war she was never going to win? She was no match for Ingram and Bunny and never would be. That's who she was and she was entitled to that much, at least. He wished he hadn't tempted her, prompted her. Subjected her to more frustration, more loss. One thing was for sure—he wouldn't do it again.

The best thing he could do was to leave before it got even worse. And again go without a trace. That way he could be the bad guy. Let her hate him. Let him take the blame. Let the naysayers be right. Love stretched the limits of what a person would do for another. He'd do that for his love. He'd go home, lick his wounds and then move forward. Like he always did. Alone. This brush with could-have-been would be the final one. Yes, a new set of memories would forever vie for his attention. Memories he'd secretly treasure like jewels for the rest of his days. Just there to remind him of what was almost possible. They'd be enough.

They'd have to be.

He tossed everything he'd brought for the trip into suitcases and called for a car and ferryboat. On the table, he noticed the drawing he'd done of Erin when everybody else was sketching trees. How much he'd enjoyed putting her likeness down on paper, the curve of her jaw, every strand of her shiny hair. But he wouldn't take it back to Tokyo with him. He'd leave his drawing, along with the love he felt for her, here in the States. As it had always been. Tucked away. Where it belonged.

Grabbing a piece of the lodge's stationery, he dashed off a short note. And folded it, plus the drawing, into an envelope. He exited his cabin, went to Erin's room and slipped it under the door, figuring she was still at the brunch. Then, making sure not to be seen, he walked out the lobby doors and slid into a limo. Just as he had slid out of one a few days before.

CHAPTER EIGHT

"*ISN'T RICH AND successful our kind of people?
I found someone rich.*"

"*For heaven's sake, Erin. You know what
your mother means. Established families.
Multigenerational wealth. You have a duty
to marry strategically and produce the next
generation of the Barclay legacy.*"

Erin's shoulders slumped. Her eyes deadened. Once again, her parents were taking the
reins away from her. They'd summoned her to
a private meeting room, irate that they hadn't
been able to find her last night after the wedding. She hadn't returned their calls or texts.
No, Mother and Father, she wanted to yell. *I
was too busy making love with Kento Yamamoto in a limo to check my phone!*

Bile crept up her esophagus. Almost as if
she was going to vomit. But it was words instead that spilled out of her with ferocity. "I

love Kento!" she exclaimed. Last night, she hadn't been able to repeat those words back to him. Too afraid to say them out loud, of what admitting them might mean. But they came bursting out of her now—she couldn't shy away from them. "I love Kento. I love him! Doesn't that mean anything?"

The tone in her voice shocked all three of them. Bunny leaned back, like she was physically threatened. *Good*, she thought, let her mother be scared. Because Erin wasn't going to be anymore. She examined them. They looked older this morning than they ever had, stuffier and completely out of touch. Ingram in a stiff shirt buttoned to the neck and Italian loafers that cost more than some people earned in a month. Bunny in a tweed jacket with coordinating slacks and a gaudy necklace.

All her mother had been concerned about when she first saw Erin at the lodge a couple of days ago was that her nails weren't done. Not her grief about her failures in relationships and the breakup with Harris. No, her mother had intimated that Erin herself was to blame for his philandering, that she had failed to hold his interest.

Her parents kept a strategically curated and orderly life. All that mattered to them were bloodlines and insulation from anything outside their bubble. Her mind flashed forwarded. Probably with a few more tries, it would be her in the tweed jacket soon, spending her days with women just like her for overpriced salad lunches picked at while passing judgment on others. Who was married to whom and who was having whose children, as if they were all merely purebred animals.

A wry, knowing smile crossed her lips. When she'd taken Kento to see those properties she liked, he was genuinely interested. Asked her questions and was impressed with her answers. Didn't think what she was saying was trivial. He made her feel like she could do anything she wanted. And didn't understand why she wasn't.

Flying up in the Space Needle with him like the sky really was theirs to navigate, that's what she was going to have. Rocking out to a band in a club if she wanted, sharing plans and schemes at a greasy-spoon diner in the middle of the night, making magnificent love with him under a shower—it was all hers if she would only take it. Kento lived and breathed freedom. And the time had finally come. Erin was going to do the same.

"You will put this to a stop right now, Erin," Ingram admonished, her mother echoing the ruling by pointing her gangly finger. "It is nothing short of ridiculous that we are repeating business that was settled years ago."

"You're right, Father," she snapped back, "it is ridiculous. Through your disgusting, unconscionable behavior, I lost him once. I'm not going to lose him again."

Strength continued to rise in her. As if she was undergoing metamorphosis into someone else. Determination swelled, unstoppable.

"Be reasonable," Ingram implored.

"Was it reasonable how you tried to pay Kento off to leave me? And was it reasonable that when he didn't take your obscene bribe, you terrorized him? Have you no humanity? A boy who grew up being teased and shamed because his parents didn't have *wealth* and *status* as defined by you and your crowd?" Her heartbeat pounded against her chest, pure and clear.

"We did what we thought was right," Bunny said feebly.

"What about the *status* of decency? The

wealth of hope Kento's parents had, daring to place him in schools with families like ours? And it turns out you two were bullies far more evil than those in the schoolyard."

"Enough," Ingram said with a tightly furrowed brow.

Again, Erin's parents looked so old and brittle to her. This life was all they knew. Actually, she felt sorry for them. She had never contemplated whether or not they were happy, whether they were in love. They weren't affectionate with each other or with her. She'd grown up in a mansion with an elevator where the three inhabitants hardly saw each other. That mansion was a jail. She was going to break out. They never would.

"You're right, Father, this is enough. I don't know if you ever had hopes or dreams, because, if you did, you never told me about them. But I'm going to take a chance on mine."

"We won't have it, Erin," Bunny yapped.

"Well, then, you won't have *me*."

"Is that a decision you're ready to make?" Ingram clicked his tongue against the roof of his mouth.

"When I tell you that I love him, that I

want to spend the rest of my life with him, that means nothing to you?"

"It sounds like you have a choice to make." Ingram's face was as rigid as stone.

The reckoning had come. All the anger expunged out of her, it was with nothing but genuine sadness that she said quietly, ultimately, "The decision isn't mine. It's yours."

Just a few tears stung Erin's eyes after the confrontation with her parents. She dabbed at them in the lobby ladies' room before heading into the lounge where the gift-opening brunch was still in session. Christy was regaling guests with the design plan for her and Lucas's dining room as she showed off the new tablecloths and napkins they'd received. An enormous array of gifts awaited placement in their new home.

Erin knew she'd been remiss in her maid of honor duties during the brunch, having been called away from Christy's side by her fuming parents. Returning to the lounge, she expected to find Kento there. She had something to tell him. Something important. Yet she scanned past the buffet tables that were now empty, past the guests who were still huddled around the newlyweds, and she couldn't spot him.

Catching Christy's eye, Erin put her hand to her heart as a gesture of apology. To which her cousin saluted and went back to swooning over her new crystal stemware and china gravy boat. It seemed as if she hadn't even noticed Erin's absence. MacKenzie sat next to the bride, filling in for the maid of honor's job of disposing of the wrapping paper and making note of which guests brought which gift.

The conversation with Erin's parents had concluded abruptly, with them telling her that if she opted to be with Kento, they would cut ties with her. She'd again reminded them that no matter how they later explained their split from their daughter, the three of them would always know that it was their choice and not hers.

Hopefulness mixed with terror mixed with confidence. Naturally, she felt uncertain. She'd allowed her parents to lord over her for twenty-eight years. It would be a whole new world for her, one where nothing was guaranteed. Well, maybe one thing was. That's what she needed to tell Kento.

As she rushed to her room to get her phone,

which she'd forgotten, her enthusiasm swirled. While no one would want it to be necessary to separate from their parents in order to fully realize their own life, in her case, she had to. The emancipation was already a relief. There was no predicting what would happen with her and Kento, but the thrill of anticipation had her flying down the lodge corridor so fast her feet weren't touching the ground. She wasn't able to say the three crucial words last night, still too repressed to utter what she knew was true and always had been. Nothing would stop her now.

After swiping the key card and opening the door, the first thing she saw was an envelope bearing the lodge's logo that had been slipped under the door. Perhaps it was checkout instructions, as the wedding party would be leaving the island in a few hours, either heading for homes in the Seattle area or boarding airplanes to their destinations. Erin bent down to pick up the envelope and used a fingernail to tear it open.

Inside was a short note along with the drawing of her that Kento had done yesterday morning for their destressing activity. While the others were sketching trees, he was depicting her. When he'd allowed the art teacher to look at it, which she turned to show to everyone, an erotic charge had sizzled through Erin. That he had been staring at her, scrutinizing her to put her likeness down on paper made her feel desirable and desired. This time, unfolding the two creases that divided the piece of paper into three sections, the air around her turned gray.

Likewise it was with dread that she then unfolded the letter. On the lodge's stationery, a precise and even handwriting she remembered from years gone by filled her with alarm.

Dear Erin,
It was fun to dream with you again after all this time. But I think we both know that wishes can't always come true.
  I'll cherish what we had until my dying day.
Farewell,
Kento

Both the note and the drawing slipped from her hands and fluttered down to the carpet. Feeling faint and unable to take a complete breath, she made it a few steps backward so that she could sit down on the edge of the bed. The discarded pieces of paper demanded her attention, and she glared at them. As if the words could magically be erased and replaced with better ones, as if the pencil sketch was merely of a tree branch after all.

Had he deserted her again? She reached over to the nightstand and picked up the lodge's phone to ring the front desk. "Kento Yamamoto's cabin, please." Her voice was so tight and strained she didn't even recognize it.

"Mr. Yamamoto has already checked out and left the property," came a reply that sounded like a robot, tinny and faraway. "Is there anything else I can help you with?"

"No." She wasn't sure if the word came out or if she had only mouthed it. She set the receiver down.

We both know that wishes can't always come true.

Of course. This hadn't been real for him. After all he'd suffered here in Seattle, much of it at her parents' hands, he'd come back for a redo fantasy. To clear his own mind. As a purge. A catharsis. A vindication. He'd reached a point in his life where he needed to set the record straight. She understood that he'd had to use her for that. There was no other way. As they tripped down memory lane, it was important to reckon, at last together, with what they had lost.

What of his declaration of love? He was only human and had gotten carried away by the romance of the island, of the wedding, of the city. Would this have ended differently if she'd told him she loved him last night? That was something she'd never know the answer to. An opportunity she'd never get back. Regret pounded through her.

Despite their flighty talk about him returning to Seattle and her traveling to Japan, the morning dawn must have enlightened him that none of that was ever going to happen. That he'd told her he loved her only in the unreal wee-hours hush that going backward in time had brought. The daylight convinced him Erin would still, as always, submit to her parents' rule that would never include him. She hadn't had a chance to explain to him the epiphanies she'd come to, conclusions made. Because of him.

Collecting the pieces of paper from the carpet, she ran her index finger slowly across the words he'd written. As if touching the letters brought her closer to him. Made him able to hear her silent plea for him to come back. To grasp that he'd been mistaken.

Only when a tear dripped onto the note did she realize that she was crying.

Maybe it was he who needed change. He'd arrived at the wedding sure that he'd never be in a serious relationship ever again. Trust was not for him, neither to give nor receive. Perhaps letting go of that was more than he could manage. It was he who was in jail. He'd proven once already that goodbyes were not his style. The message was easy to understand. *Farewell*, he'd written. She didn't know if she could *fare well* without him now that he'd returned and shown her that what might have been could still be. She held the note and sketch at arm's length so that the flowing teardrops didn't mar them. Those pieces of paper would get tucked away somewhere, but she'd hold them in her heart forever.

After lying facedown on the bed pillow until it was drenched and heavy with her sobs, she rose up to pack her luggage. Moving sluggishly, like a zombie, she carried out the motions. The original plan was that she'd return home with her parents to the Tudor monstrosity where she'd lived her lonely childhood, eating her meals in the kitchen with servants. The fiasco with Harris in Spokane still needed to be mopped up, but that was to come later. Even if she wasn't going to be granted the gift of a life with Kento, she would not go running back to her parents. She was done with them, done with the people that wouldn't sanction love and happiness.

Harris had withdrawn most of her personal savings to finance his jet-setting. Fortunately, Erin still had a little bit of protected money to keep her afloat until she figured out her next move. So instead of Seattle, she'd head to Spokane to collect her belongings there. After that, she didn't know what was around the corner. But she vowed to embrace the new beginning because Kento would have wanted her to.

Downstairs, she said her goodbyes to the wedding party. Her lip hitched up when she noticed bridesmaid Amber and groomsman Demarcus holding hands. MacKenzie and Divya were both chatting with men.

Amber saw her and winked. "'By-ee."

"'By-ee," MacKenzie echoed.

"'By-ee," Divya rang in.

"Did Kento say anything to you when he left?" she whispered into Christy's ear as she kissed her cheek.

"Only that he had an early flight scheduled. Now that I think of it, he seemed upset. Is something going on?"

"It was a beautiful wedding, cousin." Lucas grabbed her for a bear hug.

Then she stepped into the shuttle van that would take her to the ferry. Rain distorted the view out the window as they left. Chugging down the road away from the lodge, the weekend became further and further away.

Christy had said Kento was *upset* when he left. It wasn't possible that he'd overheard some of Erin's conversation with her parents, was it? How could he have? What did it matter, though? He hadn't come to her to discuss it. Once again, he'd left. He'd soon be five thousand miles from her heart, never knowing that he actually held it in the palm of his strong hand.

Once Kento boarded the boat he'd hired to ferry him across the Sound, his mind was already halfway home. As a matter of fact, he kept his eyes forward and refused to look back toward the island to what he was leaving behind. He zipped his jacket and pulled on his hood in the rain, wondering whether Erin had seen his note yet. He'd hardly known what to write, only that, this time, he *should* just leave and not linger around trying to hash things out any further. Every second, every word spoken, was just prolonging the inevitable, and he'd hate to make anything harder on Erin than it already was. There was nothing left to talk about.

The first mate handed Kento a cappuccino, for which he nodded numbly in recognition. He sipped, taking in the Seattle skyline from the bow as the boat rushed him through the waves toward the city. Proud Mount Rainier stood noble. Pike Place Market was no doubt filled with tourists enjoying how the fishmongers called out the types of their fish and then threw them across the displays to entertain the crowds. And he took a final gaze at his favorite landmark of them all, the Space Needle, whose elevators were lifting visitors up to that spectacle in the sky. He drank his cappuccino just as he drank in the city, savored it. Wished it well, knowing he might never see it again.

When he reached land, he transferred to yet another limo to take him to his jet. The opulent plane was equipped with everything a fine home would have. Once they were at a safe altitude to move around, Kento decided to take a shower. Afterward, he'd put on comfortable clothes for the long flight and concentrate on getting some work done.

A wistful sigh let loose once he was under the water. While it was quite dramatic to be flying across the Pacific as he showered, with a window looking out to the clouds and blue skies, he couldn't help but remember the two times he'd used the outdoor shower at the lodge over the weekend. The first time, he'd been alone and felt keenly aware of himself sexually, as a carnal, primitive being, spreading his arms wide and offering his body to the open elements. That's how Erin made him feel. And the second time exploring her body under the luscious gush of water until she shuddered.

He cursed himself for allowing what he'd feared would happen, that he'd return to Tokyo not having unchained himself from her. Worse still, he'd realized that he loved her, then and now, and he was ready to let go of the skepticism he'd worn as a collar for most of his life. Loving her had not been in his plans. And, as it turned out, nor was it in her parents'. So the love he'd been willing to risk himself for was not even his to have and hold.

After a couple of hours' worth of work that had piled up, he ate a meal without gusto or any sense of flavor. He systematically chewed while he stared out the window, his heart flying somewhere outside his body, too far away to grab it back. The empty thud of his torso ached. Would it always? Afterward, as he paced the cabin, the flight had never seemed longer. Attendants offered him chocolates, a cocktail, a magazine. Nothing interested him. Eventually, he put on a mindless movie that would lull him to sleep and help break up the travel time.

Another limo ride after landing and, finally, he used his key fob to open his apartment's door and slipped off his shoes. He'd returned home alone from faraway journeys many an instance but, this time, the clang of loneliness in his apartment was deafening. The verve of Tokyo made its way in through the floor-to-ceiling windows of his penthouse flat. But that didn't energize him like it had before. Instead it was a mockery of the city's promise while he stayed above it all, alone.

As he sorted through the mail that the housekeeper had neatly stacked for him, the desolation was like a prolonged scream that almost drove him mad. The kitchen had been stocked with all of the groceries he typically ordered, yet they seemed unfamiliar now; he had no connection to them. He searched online and was able to find someone's low-quality video, no doubt shot on a phone, of the rock band he and Erin had gone to see after the wedding. After they'd made wild love in the limo and before they'd eaten middle-of-the-night breakfast. The guitar chords and persistent drumbeats were the only thing that kept him from breaking down to sob, which was what he felt like doing.

The next day passed in a fog. Kento visited his parents, who were ensconced at a retirement community just outside the city. They'd eschewed his offer of a deluxe apartment in the city center like his, and it was some measure of comfort to see them well and content. Within the grounds of the facility were walking paths with colorful year-round gardens. He strolled with his mother, Hina, and his father, Matsu, who wanted to hear about the wedding.

"It was nice to see old friends," he mused.

"Did you spend time with Erin?" Hina asked, getting to the center of the matter as mothers had a knack for. He'd never told them what had happened when he first came to Tokyo to work for Uncle Riku, only explaining that he and Erin had parted after realizing they were on different paths. He didn't want them to know the disappointment he'd suffered. And caused.

"Yes, we worked well together as best man and maid of honor."

"You've never forgotten her, have you?"

"Water under the bridge, as they say."

"I don't think so, son. I can see it in your eyes."

To that, his father smiled. "Your mother is a wise woman."

"You'll be thirty soon. We couldn't be prouder of your accomplishments. But something has always told me—" Hina brought her fist to her chest and tapped "—that Erin is why you've never met a woman to settle down with."

"What's the point of anything without love?" Matsu added.

After their walk he prolonged the hugs goodbye, taking that extra moment to cherish them.

Later at the office, marketing for the Fastracc program was on schedule. But Kento wasn't, and he knew it. That night he walked aimlessly through Roppongi, where the streets were filled with an international crowd. But he couldn't dodge his own shadow.

At home, he stared at the dream catcher he'd brought back from the wedding. Holding it this way or that to observe the shadows beaming through the weblike threads. Questioning if shards of light, of energy, really had any power to affect dreams. And, if they did, begging them to stop tormenting him with sweet visions of him and Erin, hand in hand, walking through the blooming of Japan's celebrated cherry blossom trees, in a bliss that had become their reality. Had Erin taken her dream catcher home from Willminson Island, or discarded it as a disposable party favor that held no meaning? He knew he'd keep his forever.

Every minute that went by, he missed Erin more, not less. The next morning he rode his motorcycle to the hiking trails and natural beauty of peaceful Okutama, one of his favorite places outside the city. A destination he'd hoped to show Erin, because he thought she would appreciate it. Although today, he could hardly notice the sights around him because his senses were filled to the brim. With Erin. How much they laughed. That fragrant sandy-colored hair that he could bury his face in. The arch of her spine when he thrust closer and closer to her as their bodies joined in divine mating. The way they could just be together, sometimes quiet, bonding one another to the earth and to each other.

How could he have done the same thing to her a second time? Leave without confronting her, asking her, begging her, to choose him. After agreeing that they'd see each other again soon, maybe this time with him by her side she might have been able to stand up for what was fair. Instead he'd bolted again, convincing himself that was in her best interest. What if he was wrong, and he'd stolen from both of them the chance they had to start from here?

His parents were right. What was the point of anything without love? Somehow he had to right all of the wrongs. This couldn't be how things ended—with him sitting alone on his empty black leather sofa way up in the sky.

CHAPTER NINE

ONCE SHE AND her luggage were inside the Spokane town house, Erin shut the door behind her. Eyes panning left to right, it was as if she'd never been there before. Blech. It was as ugly as could be, ornamental and overdone, a ridiculously large staircase with wrought-iron railing and a carpet runner eating up the space. In a historic property, the rail would have been done in a fine wood, with the stairs made of marble. The town house was built a mere five years ago, in a supposedly traditional style that managed to be only drab.

With that staircase it was no wonder that Harris left her, she thought, knowing she was being sarcastic even to herself. Kento would have laughed at that. He might have been the only one who would have. That was one of the things she loved about him, that they could share a dark humor. The anguish of the morning replayed itself over and over again as she contemplated the antique Victorian vases that adorned the foyer table, again like this was the first time she was seeing them. The whole room was a bore. The Barclay empire could do with hiring some new decorators. Not that anything to do with her family was a concern of hers anymore. The tiny twinkling in her gut that wanted to rejoice in the fact that she'd finally set herself loose from them was squashed, because without Kento the turn of events was more bitter than sweet.

Exhausted from the journey—the van to the ferry to the car service to the airport to the taxi home after the flight—she was hungry and thirsty. Making her way to the gourmet kitchen that she and Harris had rarely used, she opened the fridge to find that the housekeeper had stocked it with food and beverages. For some reason that annoyed her, maybe because Erin hadn't asked her to. She was quite capable of going to a market and buying her own food. Something she was looking forward to doing for the rest of her life.

Nonetheless, she needed to eat before she could just go upstairs to bed and wake up to her new and uncertain life tomorrow. While the microwave heated up the pasta and vegetables she selected, she flicked on the television for company. And barely glanced at it as she chomped the meal just to be done with it.

In her bedroom, she opened her luggage. Spotting the violet maid of honor gown, she sniggered. The dress had been through a lot. Not just the wedding ceremony and reception. That piece of purple satin had ridden up the elevator of the Space Needle. Had happily spent time on the floor of the limo while she and Kento were engaged in an activity that required a different dress code—an undress code. Then the gown arrived overdressed to hear a rock band. And finally to eat a predawn breakfast before it finally got a few hours' sleep on the chair beside the bed in Kento's cabin.

Inspecting it now, she saw the hem had become soiled and frayed, no doubt from getting in and out of the limo on the wet city curbs. There was a stain on the bodice. Erin vaguely recalled spilling some coffee at the diner. And there was a bit of a tear on the side under the arm. Had Kento been overeager when he took it off her in the black-windowed privacy of the limo ride? It thrilled her to think so. What would she do, have the gown cleaned and mended? That seemed absurd. It wasn't as if she'd ever wear it again. One thing was for sure, though. She was not going to throw it away.

As she shuffled through her toiletries to get ready for bed, another reminder she'd brought home caught her eye. It was from the rehearsal dinner when they'd seen the show about Native American history. She held the dream catcher up by the loop that the guests were told could be used to hang it above their beds. The beads were weighty and the feathers smooth. Had Kento taken his back to Japan with him, or thrown it out as a meaningless party favor?

What dreams would that catcher bring now? What was to become of her? Not sorry that she'd walked out of her cruel parents' grip, the fact remained that she was a single twenty-eight-year-old with no sure future. Once she packed up here, there was nothing for her in Spokane. Would she return to Seattle? The wedding crowd and their lives there had been hers, the overprivileged offspring their families raised them to be. Without her parents, she didn't belong in that world anymore. She was no longer *their kind* of people. There was nowhere Erin could call home.

Adding self-pity to the mash-up of emotions that swirled within her, she knew she had to do this alone. Reinventing herself would be not just easier with support, but this weekend she'd come to realize that everything was so much more fulfilling when shared with someone, partnered with someone. In life and in love. Not just anyone, she corrected herself. *The* someone. Two gorounds, and yet she still ended up without him!

Kento, Kento, Kento, Kento, her brain chanted.

Please, she begged the dream catcher she clutched like her life depended on it as she crawled into bed. *Let me at least dream about him.*

Waking up in the morning after a fitful but dreamless sleep, Erin showered, dressed and had breakfast. In the clear light of day, she made a list of what she needed to do. Moving out of this awful town house was the first order of business. Someone else could deal with Harris's things; she didn't care who. She'd carry the love and loss of Kento with her for the rest of her days on earth. But not of party boy Harris, or of the other Mr. Wrongs she'd dated. They'd be easy to put behind her.

In the basement looking for boxes to pack up with, she found one that she'd stashed away because it was filled with private mementos from her university years. Carrying it up to the living room, she placed it beside one of the ornate wooden-framed sofas on the Persian rug. Not remembering where anything was kept, she riffled through a couple of drawers in the desk before she found a pair of scissors to cut through the tape sealing the box. Sitting down, she began sorting through its contents.

A couple of old sports uniforms padded the top. Followed by some trophies and certificates. Framed photos of club events. Nothing of great recognition or importance to her. In fact, she had no idea why she'd saved them. But as soon as her eyes made contact with the next item, the hairs on her arms stood on end. It was an album of photos she'd printed back then. Of her and Kento.

Tears quickly filled her eyes as she turned back the cover to see the first page. With arms around each other, they both had smiles on their faces. Kento wore shirtsleeves but with a tie, and she had on a lot of makeup. Without thinking twice, her fingertips trailed across Kento's thick hair and then his full lips.

Alternating between turning the pages and hugging the album to her chest, sobs erupted from her. The two of them barefoot at the beach. Dressed as superheroes for a Halloween party, a sneaky, sexy smile on his face. In caps and gowns on graduation day. The clarity was as bright as a sunny day. She loved Kento with all of her heart and always had. Always. Had. Since the very first day when they met in that philosophy class.

They'd been named partners, assigned to a project that required meeting several evenings at one of the campus libraries. He'd bring tangerines from his parents' store that they'd eat sitting on the stone ledge outside once they'd finished their work for the night. Conversation flowed easily—they finished each other's sentences. He wasn't like the people she'd been surrounded by, closed-minded and always measuring what others thought. Kento had big opinions and even bigger ideas, never censoring himself. And once he sneaked a kiss under the lamppost after a stimulating night of exchanging theories, they became inseparable. As they should be.

In an instant, agony turned angry. How could he have walked out on her again? He'd professed his love but hadn't given her the time to make her move. He refused to have faith in her. For the second time! Of course, she understood that he assumed her parents would get what they wanted in the end— after all, he didn't yet know she was ready to leave holding his hand. Did he think he was doing her some kind of favor by simply abandoning her again? How could he have not comprehended that was the last thing she needed?

Oh, was she going to give him a piece of her mind! Read him the riot act! And not over the phone or text or email, either. If she had to be the one to step up, fine. So be it. This was life or death as far as she was concerned. Nothing could be more worth fighting for. And so much time had already been wasted. He'd soon see what she was made of. The marching orders had come.

She knew what she needed to do and sprang into action. Swapping out the maid of honor outfits, soiled gown included, Erin repacked her suitcase with clean clothes and called for a driver.

Narita Airport was bright and bustling when Erin deplaned after the long flight from Seattle. It stunned her to step foot on solid ground after arrival, to believe that she was really here. Without talking herself out of it, she'd simply booked and boarded a flight to Tokyo. Unfinished business at the wedding weekend had prompted her to go, even when phone calls to discuss her plan went unanswered. In the boldest move she had ever made, she traveled alone to this mighty city across the Pacific on a mission to get what she could no longer live without.

She'd spent the flight studying the Japanese language lessons she'd downloaded before leaving. Sure, she'd only remember a couple of basic words, but at least it was a start. Airport signs for the baggage claim and ground transportation were written in Japanese and in English, some in Chinese and Korean as well. With their help, she was easily able to locate her luggage and get a taxi.

A mixture of exhilaration and fear greeted her when the cab dropped her off in front of the hotel she'd reserved in the busy Shibuya ward. She stood for a moment on the street, hardly able to comprehend the scene. The crowds at Shibuya Crossing were massive, the intersection far bigger than Times Square in New York. Tens of thousands of people trod through every day. It was nicknamed the Scramble, and she understood why. Businesses were bustling. Building exteriors were stacked with flickering ads, giant video screens and so many lights—more than the eye could even take in. The pulse of the entire area was pounding. Erin had never seen anything like it.

Entering her hotel, she was greeted with bows by the welcome desk staff. Erin knew there were specific rituals regarding the practice of bowing she'd need to learn, but a tourist could get away with a nod of the head and still be considered polite. "*Konnichiwa*. Hello," one of the staff members said to her as she handed over her identification and credit card.

Her room was decorated with tasteful earth tones. Recessed lighting on a dimmer gave options, and the minimalist room had been nicely divided into work and sleep space. It was afternoon, and Erin planned to spend the day getting acclimated before beginning her business in the morning. That business being taking her place next to the man she loved.

But knowing she was in the same city as him now, she couldn't wait any longer. When she tapped into her phone, the call to Kento went straight to voice mail, as had the two she'd tried before leaving Washington. It was disappointing and alarming that there was no reply. Maybe he hadn't received the messages. The phone number he'd given her had a Seattle area code—perhaps he was only using that one for the wedding and didn't check the voice mail. She'd hoped not to have to get anyone in Seattle involved, but she'd call Lucas tomorrow if she had to. Another very logical consideration dawned on her. He could have heard her messages and decided not to respond. When he made up his mind about something, he acted on it. Conviction—yet another thing she loved about him.

She'd known what she was doing by getting on that plane. He'd told her that he loved her and she hadn't assured him that she did, too, in return. She needed to say it in person.

There was nothing to lose now except him, and she wasn't going to let that piece of her past repeat itself. He might not be good at goodbye, but Erin was going to give him one heck of a hello. As many hellos as it took, as a matter of fact.

Restless, she left her hotel to explore the busy streets. Shops, restaurants, nightclubs and bars took up every bit of space. She wandered a bit away from the commercial blocks thronged with humans, curious to see where residents lived and to begin to envision a life in this city. Weaving this way and that, she found a city park, tranquil green space that was a quiet oasis from the throb. The small park was rimmed by private homes, single-family residences as opposed to the many high-rises and apartment buildings.

The For Sale sign written in several languages in front of one of the properties caught her eye. Punching the Realtor's code that was provided into her phone, she learned that the two-story wooden home had been built in 1924. At twenty-five hundred square feet, it would be considered large for the populated inner-city neighborhood. The architecture of the simple home was beautiful, and the adjacent park was a huge asset. Erin wondered if the little germ of interest she'd always had in historic properties could grow here—a possibility she'd never considered.

After wandering for hours, she was hungry. Near her hotel were many restaurants that offered menus in English or with photos of the food so that a visitor need only point to what they wanted. She had the freshest assortment of sushi she'd ever tasted and watched from a window table as the city went by.

This was already the riskiest thing she'd ever done, flying halfway across the world toward complete uncertainty. But this was her now, one way or another. Although she refused to acknowledge a future without Kento, her life was finally starting. It was scary. She accepted that.

Following a hot shower in the smooth stone of the hotel bathroom, she checked her phone. No messages. Okay, she promised herself. Tomorrow would be a brand-new day.

Naturally, the first thing Erin did when she woke up for the first time in Tokyo was check her messages. Still none. Since it was a business day, she assumed that Kento would be going in to work, so she would head to

NIRE. Showing up to his office was going to be a shock. She hoped it would be a good one.

NIRE occupied six floors of a green glass–windowed building in Akihabara, a high-tech mecca with shops that served fandom cultures—entire stores dedicated to fictional characters, video games and electronics. After Erin rode a lightning-fast elevator to the NIRE offices, the doors opened to a reception area, which Erin stepped into. A beautiful woman in a blue suit bowed from behind a check-in desk, where a sign in a signature font read *NIRE*. Erin had meant to ask Kento over the weekend what NIRE stood for, but she hadn't had the chance.

"I'm here to see Kento Yamamoto," Erin stated after bowing her head in return.

"I'm sorry," the receptionist answered quickly, "Mr. Yamamoto's schedule is only by appointment. He is very busy." It made sense that he had a gatekeeper. Perhaps more than one. Erin began to worry how she was going to make her way into Kento's inner chamber, where he was no doubt protected from unwanted interruption.

"Could you get a message to him for me,

please? We are old friends." That was the best and most important description she could think of. An old friend who came to see him, if she could get through the barriers. A half dozen glass doors led to different corridors.

"I can relay a message to his assistant." The blue-suited receptionist stretched out her hand as if to receive an actual paper message. "Mr. Yamamoto will let us know if he wishes us to contact you."

Erin hadn't conceived of being refused access like this, although she should have. Obviously as the CEO of a huge corporation, Kento's time and security were carefully guarded. Her face got hot. Nerves began to get the best of her as she searched through her purse for a piece of paper or something to handwrite a note on. What she found seemed only too appropriate.

It was Kento's drawing of her from Lucas and Christy's wedding morning. She wanted to be up front and not waste another precious moment, so she wrote on the back.

I've come to tell you *aishiteru*.
I love you.

As soon as the drawing was handed to him, and not arriving through the postal mail, he'd realize that she was here. At least she'd know right away where she stood. Hopefully he'd burst through one of the doors and into her arms.

"Thank you." The receptionist offered another bow after receiving the folded drawing with two hands. They both stood still. Finally she asked Erin, "Is there anything further?"

"No. I'll wait for Mr. Yamamoto's response."

"I'm sorry. This is a waiting area for people who have appointments today."

Erin knew that there could be hackers, spies and all sorts of unwelcome visitors to a company like Kento's, so she understood the need for regulations. Still, though, tears burned behind her eyes as she nodded once again to the receptionist before returning to the elevator and pressing its call button.

"Thank you." The words came out of Kento's mouth in slow motion as he unfolded the piece of paper Emiko had just handed him after she relayed that someone claiming to be a friend had stopped by the office. When he unfolded the note, he couldn't believe his eyes. "How did this get here?" he demanded. How on earth could the drawing of Erin that he'd slipped under her door on Willminson Island be in his hands right now? His pulse sped, wanting more information.

Emiko confirmed the conclusion that was taking shape in his head. "Ms. Barclay delivered it herself."

He wanted to be angry at his staff for not letting the special guest in, but they'd have no way of knowing that Erin Barclay was, and would always be, more than welcome wherever he was. Emiko bowed deeply from the waist in her boss's presence and then turned to leave.

Erin was in Tokyo? How could that be? Over the course of his years here, there had to have been hundreds of times when Kento saw something on a Tokyo street or saw a scene in a movie or ate a food that he wanted to share with her. The distance to Seattle never seemed greater than it did when he was missing her, which he'd done so much of. He stared again at the note she'd written on the back of the drawing.

I've come to tell you *aishiteru.*
I love you.

She loved him. He took more air in one breath than he had in the past hundred. All of a sudden his lungs were completely open, the inhale and exhale flowing unforced and natural. Erin was in Japan and she loved him! That changed everything. Guesses popped into his mind about how she'd gotten herself here. A far cry from what he'd overheard of her conversation with her parents at the gift-opening brunch that sent him packing, deciding for both of them how best to finally end the cycle they'd been on for far too long.

In his desk drawer, he found the burner phone with the Seattle number that he'd tossed aside after he got back from the wedding. There were three messages on the voice mail, all from Erin. She explained only that she had something to say to him in person so she was getting on a plane, each message sounding a little more desperate than the one before. It hadn't occurred to him to check the phone once he got back.

As it happened, he'd reached a decision of his own. That in a couple of days, after some high-level meetings he needed to stay in town for, he was going to fly back to Seattle. Because he'd never rest until he looked Erin in the eye and apologized for deserting her not once, but twice. Begging on his knees if he had to in order to make her see that her parents couldn't deny her love and happiness. That the life she and he could have together would be worth the cost. The note and the fact that she was here had him churning with optimism that she'd already made her choice.

Where was she now? Perhaps worried that she hadn't been able to see him. When he tapped the phone number he had for her, the call went to a mailbox, where her lush voice instructed him to leave a message. "My staff just told me you'd come by. I am so sorry you weren't let in. Meet me at the Hachikō statue at noon."

After having a driver rush him to his destination, Kento couldn't get out of the car fast enough. He didn't know if or when Erin would retrieve his phone message, but he wanted to get to the meeting spot as soon as possible. As usual, many people were gathered near the statue, taking photos with Japan's most famous dog depicted in bronze.

Those clear breaths that had given him such certainty after seeing Erin's note were spiky now. He wouldn't exhale easily again until he saw her. He didn't want to get too far ahead of himself, but the fact that she was in his city made him speculate that she had gone against her parents' wishes, and that alone filled him with pride. He could hardly imagine how difficult that must have been for her, if that's what had come to pass.

Finally, the head of dusty-colored hair he'd known for so long became visible. "Erin," he yelled as he ran toward her, darting around people this way and that to get closer. "Erin!"

Once she turned her head and spotted him, a huge smile swept across her face, letting him know that the woman he loved was going to be his in the end. When he reached her, he kissed her face over and over again, her cheeks, her lips, her forehead, her eyelids.

"Kento."

"How can this be? How is that you're here?"

"Why did you leave me at the wedding?"

Wow, she wasn't mincing words.

"I saw you talking to your parents and knew…"

"Knew what? Did you hear us?"

"Only a little bit. What I heard was that you and I were still the impossibility we always were."

"Well, then, you didn't hear everything I said to them. Why didn't you wait?"

"I was trying to make it easier for us to say goodbye."

"Hey, Yamamoto. I'm not saying goodbye. You got that? I'm never saying goodbye. I made a big enough mistake after the wedding not telling you I loved you. I'm never going to let a day go by that I don't say it again."

He took her hand in his and kissed her palm. "That's the best thing I've ever heard in my life. Come here." A big, long hug in the center of the fast-moving city brought his breath back to sure and even. He positioned them so that they could take a selfie with the famous Akita statue.

"What's the story of the dog, anyway?"

"Hachikō used to wait here every day for his owner to come up from the railway station after work. Even after the owner died, the dog still came every day. For nine more years. Every day for nine years. Until he himself died."

"A symbol of loyalty."

"Of not giving up."

Kento ducked them into a café, where he ordered tea. They explained to each other what had happened after the wedding. Erin told him that her parents would have nothing to do with her anymore. That she was going to create her own path, one alongside his. "I want you to see this home I found for sale. I think I want to buy it."

That was his woman. Someone who was ready to embrace chance, to find her destiny, to look herself in the mirror. "I can't wait."

More kisses and excitement followed as Kento told her ten places in Asia he wanted to take her to see, followed by ten more.

"Hey, I never asked you something."

"What, my love?" he responded with a brush to her hair.

"You've never told me, what does the name of your company mean? Is NIRE some kind of acronym?"

Pulling a pen from his jacket pocket, he wrote the four letters big and bold on a napkin. And then held the napkin up toward the window so that she could see them written backward in the reflection.

"E-R-I-N," she read aloud, and then her mouth dropped open. "What? After all this time I'm finding out that I've lived in Tokyo all along?"

"You see? Even when we were apart, we were together."

"And we always will be." She reached her hand to his face and brought him close. *"Aishiteru,* Kento."

*"Aishiteru…*my heart."

* * * * *

*If you enjoyed this story,
check out these other great reads from
Andrea Bolter*

Captivated by Her Parisian Billionaire
His Convenient New York Bride
The Prince's Cinderella
The Italian's Runaway Princess

All available now!